GIRL FORGOTTEN

A DETECTIVE KAITLYN CARR MYSTERY

KATE GABLE

BYRD BOOKS LLC

COPYRIGHT

Proofreaders:

Julie Deaton, Deaton Author Services, https://www.facebook.com/jdproofs/

Renee Waring, Guardian Proofreading Services, https://www.facebook.com/GuardianProofreadingServices

Cover Design: Kate Gable

Visit my website at www.kategable.com

BE THE FIRST TO KNOW ABOUT MY UPCOMING SALES, NEW RELEASES AND EXCLUSIVE GIVEAWAYS!

Want a Free book? Sign up for my Newsletter!

Sign up for my newsletter:

https://www.subscribepage.com/kategableviplist

Join my Facebook Group:
https://www.facebook.com/groups/833851020557518

Bonus Points: Follow me on BookBub and Goodreads!

https://www.goodreads.com/author/show/21534224.Kate_Gable

ABOUT KATE GABLE

Kate Gable loves a good mystery that is full of suspense. She grew up devouring psychological thrillers and crime novels as well as movies, tv shows and true crime.

Her favorite stories are the ones that are centered on families with lots of secrets and lies as well as many twists and turns. Her novels have elements of psychological suspense, thriller, mystery and romance.

Kate Gable lives near Palm Springs, CA with her husband, son, a dog and a cat. She has spent more than twenty years in Southern California and finds inspiration from its cities, canyons, deserts, and small mountain towns.

She graduated from University of Southern California with a Bachelor's degree in Mathematics. After pursuing graduate studies in mathematics, she switched gears and got her MA in Creative Writing and English from Western New Mexico University and her PhD in Education from Old Dominion University.

Writing has always been her passion and obsession. Kate is also a USA Today Bestselling author of romantic suspense under another pen name.

Write her here:

Kate@kategable.com

Check out her books here:

www.kategable.com

Sign up for my newsletter:
https://www.subscribepage.com/kategableviplist

Join my Facebook Group:
https://www.facebook.com/groups/833851020557518

Bonus Points: Follow me on BookBub and Goodreads!

https://www.bookbub.com/authors/kate-gable

https://www.goodreads.com/author/show/21534224.Kate_Gable

amazon.com/Kate-Gable/e/B095XFCLL7
facebook.com/kategablebooks
bookbub.com/authors/kate-gable
instagram.com/kategablebooks

ALSO BY KATE GABLE

Detective Kaitlyn Carr Psychological Mystery series

Girl Missing (Book 1)

Girl Lost (Book 2)

Girl Found (Book 3)

Girl Taken (Book 4)

Girl Forgotten (Book 5)

Gone Too Soon (Book 6)

Gone Forever (Book 7)

Whispers in the Sand (Book 8)

Girl Hidden (FREE Novella)

Detective Charlotte Pierce Psychological Mystery series

Last Breath

Nameless Girl
Missing Lives
Girl in the Lake

ABOUT GIRL FORGOTTEN

☆☆☆☆☆ *"Gripping! Fascinating mystery thriller filled with intriguing characters and lots of twists and turns!" (Goodreads)*

A young mother just starting her life over after a bad divorce is found murdered in the Los Angeles River. The prime suspects are her ex-husband, a member of a ruthless motorcycle gang, and a new boyfriend, a surfer with a mysterious past. It's up to **Detective Kaitlyn Carr** to find out who did it.

Back in Big Bear Lake, Kaitlyn's sister's disappearance becomes a cold case and and her friend's murder goes unsolved. But Kaitlyn refuses to stop looking for her little sister.

The town where she grew up is full of secrets and Kaitlyn must confront what really happened to her father in order to find her sister.

Will Kaitlyn be able to face the truth about her family's past or will her sister remain lost forever?

This is the LAST and FINAL book focusing on Kaitlyn's sister's disappearance.

This suspenseful thriller is perfect for fans of James Patterson, Leslie Wolfe, Lisa Regan, L. T. Vargus and Karin Slaughter. It has mystery, angst, a bit of romance and family drama.

Praise for Kate Gable's Girl Missing Series

☆☆☆☆☆"Gripping! This book was a great read. I found a new author that I enjoy and I can't wait to read the rest of the series! " *(Goodreads)*

☆☆☆☆☆ "The twists come at you at breakneck pace. Very suspenseful." *(Goodreads)*

☆☆☆☆☆ "I really enjoyed the ins and outs of the storyline, it kept me reading so that I could find out how the story would turn out. And the ending was a major shocker, I never saw it coming. I truly recommend this book to everyone who loves mysteries and detective stories." *(Goodreads)*

☆☆☆☆☆" I loved it. One of the best books I've ever read." - Amazon review

☆☆☆☆☆ "I couldn't put the book down I give it a thumbs up and I would recommend it to other readers" *(Goodreads)*

☆☆☆☆☆ "Another great book in the Kaitlyn Carr series! I am so drawn into these books. I love that they are not just about Kaitlyn's search for her sister but also about a case she is working on. I can't wait for the final book in the series!" *(Goodreads)*

1

Sometimes if I've had too much of people, I like to go out into the desert, which has been a place of reflection for centuries. I like to come out here and breathe in the crisp air, feel the warmth of the sun on my shoulders and just forget about the world for a while.

Los Angeles is basically a desert, with very limited water resources and just a little bit away from Palm Springs. I have the day off and I should probably spend it in bed doing nothing, relaxing, that kind of thing.

But for some reason, I don't want to.

I get into my car, blast some music and two and a half hours later, I find myself walking on the dry land, surrounded by mountains, reaching for the sky.

I have been here a few times, each time exploring a different hike. This time, I head to the waterfall in Tahquitz Canyon. It's about a half mile walk and I scramble up the trail over the big boulders and jagged rocks.

The pamphlet up front said that I could see mountain sheep out here, but it's around ten a.m. and I know that most wildlife like to take naps during the middle of the day.

Families and couples pass me, holding hands, helping their children along the way to hear the sounds of nature. There's a creek running down past me. The humidity is hovering around ten percent. I'm not used to the harshness of desert air, but the sky is piercing blue. The waterfall is visible from about fifty feet away, and I walk up to the crystal clear pool of water into which it dumps.

Somebody's trying to scramble a large, perfectly round boulder out in the distance. He pushes off nearby walls and launches himself to the top.

I wade into the water.

I'm not wearing a bathing suit, but I go waist deep anyway. I figure my shorts and underwear are going to dry by the time I get back to the car.

After taking a few pictures and selfies, I sit down on a jagged rock and enjoy the moment.

Luke, my boyfriend, is in Wichita now, spending time with his family. I was invited to go and I thought that I would, but when the time came, I had pushed him away.

Upset and annoyed with me, he went by himself, probably offering his family a tepid excuse, or perhaps, not saying anything at all.

I'm angry with myself, annoyed and frustrated. He's been the one good thing that has happened to me.

He was the one who came in and picked me up and put up with all of my crap, broke down all of my defenses. But then when it came down to it, I pushed him away.

I don't know why this relationship is so hard for me, except that's a lie.

I know perfectly well. My family life has been less than ideal to use coded psychological language. My parents had a toxic co-dependent relationship and my mom and I have always butted heads about practically everything. When my sister went missing, all of our scars that had been buried deep inside were brought up to the surface.

I'd packed my bag to go to Wichita. But instead of getting on that plane, I ended up here in the desert, searching for something that I know exists fifteen hundred miles away.

Why couldn't I get on that plane?

Why couldn't I go and be there for him?

The way he has been there for me.

As I drive out of the canyon, I see the areas of green leading into the dark brown rocks of the surrounding mountains and the palm trees growing in the valley below.

The few times that I've been here in the height of winter, the mountaintops have been painted white, capped with snow all around giving it a particularly magnificent look against the ocean of palm trees.

I stop to eat at a restaurant on Indian Canyon Boulevard. It's highly rated on Yelp and the food doesn't disappoint. I have some waffles with Nutella, a plate of blueberries and strawberries, the fluffiest pancakes, and the most delicious crepe I've ever had. It's smothered in creme anglaise, which has somehow been made into vegan creme anglaise.

As I savor my food, I consider staying the night. I have my bag packed and nothing to get back to.

With a few days off work, why not?

Except that coming here, being on a trip at all, makes me feel incredibly guilty. It's worse than I have ever felt before. I should be in Kansas with Luke. He did nothing wrong and was just kind and sweet, helping me through a difficult time.

I should get past all of my issues and actually commit.

But it's not like I'm out here looking for another date. Not at all.

It's just that it's hard to compare being with someone to being alone. I like this misery, this darkness that envelops me, brooding and being slightly dissatisfied all the time.

It started even before Violet disappeared.

I thought I was just being cool. I thought that was just what you did in LA. Stayed single.

Didn't commit, not really think about the future.

There're fifty year olds acting like they're twenty-five and sixty and seventy year olds acting like they're thirty.

A part of the problem is that I never imagined myself being a mother, a wife. I always imagined being a detective or heck, even a writer. I managed to finish the book that I was working on thanks largely to Luke and his constant support, telling me that I could do it and believing in me. No one else has done that for me before.

I shouldn't compare but I can't help myself. When my ex, Thomas, found out about me wanting to be a writer, he thought it was a joke.

Writers know things, and in his eyes I was an idiot. He didn't care that I had scored higher on all of my exams than he did. He thought that the only reason I got promoted was because the department had a quota to fill.

The truth is that I worked harder than Thomas. I was smarter and more committed and he scored better. But he still had a job because the department is still a boys club. He was friends with the higher ups and they saw him as younger versions of themselves, so he got promoted.

People like Thomas got the cases the people like me didn't.

Luke wasn't anything like that.

He wanted to spend the rest of his life with me; he wanted me to be his wife. He said that, in not so many words.

Okay. I should be happy.

I am not with some ass who hurts me. I am with a guy who loves me and supports me no matter what. He doesn't call me names or make me feel bad. He has never even raised his voice at me.

I have to quit comparing Luke to the worst thing that ever happened to me. He deserves much better than that.

2

I take my time at the restaurant, hanging around longer than I probably should. I ask for a second helping of tea and then another, decaf this time because I don't want to stay up late.

When I finish the last of it, I pay the bill, give the waitress a very generous tip, and get in my car.

I consider spending the night.

My bag is packed in the trunk, and it would be nice not to drive all the way home, but old thoughts start to creep back, and I know that it would be better to go back home and get back to work rather than hang around here as an idling tourist waiting for something.

What exactly?

What is holding me back?

I wanted to go on a hike. I did. It was beautiful. Breathtaking views, different from back home. A little bit of city in sight, but not much else.

For a moment, I think about living here. There's a lot less traffic, and the whole Coachella valley can be crisscrossed in what is it, half an hour? That sounds pretty good to me right about now.

Luke calls and I ask about his mom and his trip, but there's a coldness that exists between us.

A lot of pauses.

He asks me what I'm doing and I'm tempted to lie, but I don't.

"You went all the way to Palm Springs?" he asks. "Why?"

"Just felt like it. Needed to clear my head."

"You could have come here."

This is a sly comment, revealing the truth of how he feels.

"I get it. I know. I'm sorry."

"You're not going to fly out?" he asks.

"I don't know," I mumble.

"Why not? I mean, you took the days off. Just come. I can get you a flight."

I hesitate, and before I can say no, he says, "Fine. I've got to go," and hangs up the phone.

Still hesitating, I pull out my laptop and check for flights out of the Palm Springs Airport.

There's one for later this afternoon. It stops in Dallas and costs about triple what my old flight did, but riding the high of excitement, I pull out my credit card. I have just enough time to get to the airport. I book the trip for five days, getting in late tonight and coming back on Thursday.

On the flight, my heart beats out of my chest until I turn up the music and put my thoughts elsewhere.

"Everything is going to be fine," I say over and over to myself. I don't bring anything for checked baggage, just a carry-on and my backpack with my laptop, iPad, and chargers.

When I walk out through the baggage claim toward the car rental, the humidity of the Midwest hits me like a ton of bricks. The air feels thick enough to swim through, and I struggle to breathe. No matter how hot the summers tend to get in Los Angeles, let alone in Palm Springs, the sheer thickness of the air here takes me by complete surprise.

I'm drenched in sweat as I head to the car rental building and then immediately freeze from the air conditioning inside. I get the cheapest car they have, a

Kia Forte, but it handles well and zooms around quickly.

I keep debating whether or not I should call Luke before arriving, but the more time that passes, the more reluctant I am to call him, and so I don't. I have his address from an email that he sent me a while ago, so I head straight there.

Luke is staying at his mom's farmhouse. He grew up in the suburbs going to nice big, Blue Ribbon schools, but as soon as he graduated, his mom bought a white farmhouse with a wrap-around porch, and she and his dad remodeled it themselves.

"They had no experience in that sort of thing, and that was part of the fun," Luke said and winked at me when he told me the story.

But he grew up in the blandness of the suburbs, one of those new construction, cookie-cutter homes that I've actually always wanted to live in.

I, on the other hand, grew up in what could be called a historic home in a small town with leaky pipes, poor insulation, wood paneling, and all of the other charms of vintage house living, and I have no interest in going through any of that again.

Nearing my destination, I see a quintessential white farmhouse in the distance, perched on what I can't exactly call a hill. There are two big weeping willows with a tire swing out front and I feel like I've entered another world.

Out here, it's pitch black all around except for a few floodlights leading up the road. I see the light in each of the rooms and shadows of people gathered on the porch. I lean closer and see that they're actually *rocking* in their rocking chairs.

My headlights flood the dirt road, and out in the distance someone on the porch gets up and looks in my direction. Few people come unannounced this way. I wish there were some way I could tell him that it's me. The shadow stands up and heads toward me. I can't tell whether it's Luke or his brother, who has a very similar, wiry frame, only a little bit shorter than he is.

There's a gate blocking my path the rest of the way up, and I get out to pull it to one side, double-checking the number carved into the wood in the corner and make sure that all five of them match the number that I have on the email in my phone.

Yes, this is the correct place. I drive all the way up to the house where two men, their legs wide apart and arms by their sides, stand on the porch. I can't see their faces and I wonder if they're glaring. Once I turn off the high beams and get out of the car, one of the men jumps over the steps toward me, pulling me into his arms.

"What are you doing here?" Luke asks, kissing my forehead, cheek, and eventually my lips.

When our mouths touch, I know that I've made the right decision, and all the nervousness and anxiety somehow magically melts away.

"Sam, this is Kaitlyn, my girlfriend," Luke introduces me without the slightest hesitation.

I take his brother's hand as he gives me a firm handshake, but not too firm, like he's trying too hard. The two of them look like twins.

Luke is a little taller and younger, but they're even dressed in similar ratty t-shirts and well-worn baseball caps to match. Luke's wearing cargo pants that I don't think I've seen since my college days in the 2000s, while Sam is dressed in loose-fitting jeans that hang low on his hips.

"What are you doing here? You said you weren't going to come."

"Yeah, well, I had a little bit of a change of plans. I wanted to see you," I whisper and kiss him again.

"Okay, you two love birds. Come on in. I'm sure Mom is eager to meet you."

I bite my lower lip and look up at Luke with a tentative smile. He tilts his head. "Listen, I can't promise anything. She was eagerly awaiting your visit before. Now, I have no idea."

"Seriously?" My heart drops into the pit of my stomach.

"No, of course not. She's going to be so happy to see you," he says, waving his arms in my direction like I'm an idiot. I laugh, not being quite ready for it but appreciating the joke nonetheless.

The farmhouse is beautiful. It was built in the 1890s, and the Gavinsons bought it at an auction for $95,000 when it was dilapidated and completely forgotten.

This has been their project over the last fifteen years and a place where Luke spent many of his summers from college working on the electrical system, the plumbing, and anything else that they needed.

It's after eleven p.m., and the family is still up. I meet Sam's wife, Miranda, their one-year-old baby, who just woke up for a midnight snack from the boob, and Mr. and Mrs. Gavinson, Luke's parents. There's freshly made pecan pie on the dining room table, which has been lovingly designed with an eclectic combination of furniture and interior design details.

Miranda tells me all about it, as she had a hand in it. Some pieces, like the table, they found at an antique mall; it's from the nineteen hundreds, while the chairs are mid-century and the clock is from five years ago, but designed by a retro company and styled as if it's from the 1950s. You wouldn't think from hearing about it that it would all complement each other, but somehow the colors, the textures, and the designs do just that. They bring out the best in the space and make it incredibly comfortable and pleasing to the eye.

Miranda is a few years younger than me and is a kindergarten teacher who loves children. Sam is a physical therapist who recently opened his own office and hired two assistants to work under him. They live in Kansas City, Missouri, not too far away, but Miranda loves Southern California and has visited her brother-in-law on numerous occasions. Luke's mom has rosy, red cheeks and thin, practically translucent skin.

She has wide-set eyes, poofy, reddish auburn hair, and the kindest smile I've ever seen. Her arm is still in a brace, and we talk a little bit about her shoulder surgery and how much she has struggled over the last few months in not being able to do everything that she normally does.

I get the feeling that she's a very active woman who likes to go on walks, exercises four times a week, as well as runs the bakery that she had opened after retiring from being an accountant for 30 years.

"Well, after we finished the construction on this house, I had to do something. I mean, there are many hours in the day. I volunteered. I worked at the library. The renovations on the farmhouse were already coming along well. But I still needed more in my day. I've always loved to bake, and I've always wanted to run a bakery. We figured if we made a little bit over breaking even that would be fine, and it would only be open for the morning rush anyway, if there would even be a rush all the way out here."

"So, what happened?" I ask.

Luke puts his hands around her shoulders and gives her a wicked smile. "What happened is that this bakery became the talk of the town, and people drive out forty-five, sixty, ninety minutes just to get her scones, let alone the wedding cakes."

"I actually had to hire people," she says, waving her arm in my direction. "Can you believe that? I mean, it was just going to be me and it was just going to be for fun, but it really took off."

"That's because you put all your love into it," Sam says, giving her a kiss on the forehead.

Mr. Gavinson, Ross, as he asks me to call him, sits at the head of the table and looks at his family, his sons being the spitting image of him. He's tall and lanky and has worked as an engineer his whole life.

"Do you help her in the bakery, Ross?" I ask.

"He can't come within two feet of it. That's my domain," Bea, short for Beatrix, says, putting her hand up in protest.

"So you're just home all alone, enjoying your retirement and the house?" I ask with a smile.

"I wish."

"No, you don't." Sam shakes his head at his father.

I look at Luke for an explanation.

"Dad's always been into rebuilding cars. It's been an obsession of his. Classic cars mainly. So, after he retired we, of course, got him a 1952 Ford Mustang that was supposed to take him five years to fix up in between playing golf and all the other stuff that you're supposed to do in retirement."

"You mean like drink and watch inordinate amounts of cable news? No, thank you," Ross says, looking over at Bea in that loving way that I've only seen people do on television and in movies.

"He finished that car in nine months and sold it for, what was it?" Luke says. "Ten times the cost of the parts, and then immediately got himself another project. So now he restores. Now he's got a shop out back, even built a big garage to protect it from the elements in the winter and summer, and he works out there all the time."

"Do you have any assistants?" I ask.

"Actually, I'm interviewing three people tomorrow. Business is growing. I don't want it to grow so far that I end up doing all the paperwork and none of the fun stuff, but yeah, it's going to be good to have a little bit of help."

They laugh and take sips of their beer and bourbon. I'm not sure how long they've been drinking, but no one is intoxicated at all, despite the time of night. Half an hour later, Bea and Ross go upstairs, each giving me a warm embrace and a kiss on the cheek.

"You are so much more wonderful than Luke even said," Bea whispers into my ear.

"Luke is lucky to have you," Ross says, giving me a peck on the cheek and a squeeze of the hand.

When Teddy finishes his snack, Sam and Miranda wave goodbye and disappear into the guest room downstairs, and Luke looks over at me and raises his eyebrows for a moment.

"So, what do you think? As scary as you thought they would be?"

3

KELLY

I drop Mikey, my four-year-old son, off at my ex-husband's and go on a drive. I don't intend to do that, but I have the day off from work and a lot of time on my hands. This is the first official drop-off after our divorce.

Sonny was so insistent that the breakup be amicable at first, but then it got increasingly more contentious once we started separating the pots and pans of our life. I know I've made lots of mistakes. I paid for everything for a long time, allowing Sonny to go from job to job, sticking with nothing in particular. Meanwhile, I took care of Mikey during the days and worked nights as a nurse.

Sonny was against daycare even before I could afford it. He was against preschool. He didn't want to be a stay-at-home dad either. He expected me to be a full-time mother and put money on the table, or perhaps he just expected us to live off what he made as a third-rate drug dealer.

We'd met in high school, and though I went to Cal State Los Angeles, he kept telling me to drop out. He had no plans for his future and he thought that I didn't need to do any work away from home. I stayed with Sonny for way too long.

I know this. I should have dumped him on our third date when he told me what a great mother I would make. Life was hard for me.

I don't have any family. I grew up in foster care. At eighteen, I was practically put out on the street, and if they hadn't done that I would have run away.

Sonny paid attention to me in high school when no one else did. I thought he loved me. As the year passed, he ended up being my family. I didn't have many friends. But Sonny did. We socialized mainly with his motorcycle club friends who spent all their time selling drugs while their women worked as nurses, nursing assistants, and the occasional porn star.

Sonny's family is tight. They uphold a code of honor, and they live according to the laws of the street where loyalty is number one and nothing else matters. That's why his brother is serving seven to ten years upstate for armed robbery, doing everybody's time. To turn on your brother is the worst crime you can commit. And if he had talked, he would have been killed.

I dropped off Mikey at Sonny's mother's home, where Sonny still lives. She's the main caregiver and I know that I will be bound to that family for life unless something changes.

They have made threats and even broken into my apartment on a few occasions, but I can't really prove any of this. Besides, what would be the point?

If I didn't have Mikey, I would get into the car and drive as far away as possible, all the way to the Oregon coast, maybe the Canadian border or Florida. I like the idea of the last one the most. I imagine the two of us somewhere warm with manatees, dolphins, and warm water.

I grab onto the steering wheel of my 2003 Chrysler Sebring, and I open the windows because the air conditioning doesn't work. The closest beach to my house is Santa Monica. But Sonny's motorcycle brothers are known to meander there trying to find new lost souls to sell Fentanyl and Oxycontin to on the Venice boardwalk.

Instead, I head south. I don't want a beach with a lot of people, or a city. I want something out of the way where I can be alone with my thoughts. I drive all the way down to Oceanside, staying on the freeway for as long as possible. I don't play any music. I just let myself get lost in my thoughts.

When I arrive, I park on one of the side streets and change into a bathing suit in the car. I put my long sleeve dress over it. I know the water will be frigid, hovering somewhere around sixty degrees. It doesn't get warm the way it does on the East Coast, or so I've heard, mainly because the current comes all the way up from Alaska. But as far as the west coast of the U.S. goes, the water is the warmest right around here and San Diego.

I walk through the sand, out into the water, and stare at the horizon. The sky is overcast, full of clouds. The sea is menacing. I take off my shoes and dip my feet in. The chill zaps me at first, freezing my toes, but as I walk and get acclimated, it starts to feel good.

"I need to get away from him," I say to myself, staring out at the horizon. "I need to save myself and Mikey."

I WALK FURTHER into the frigid water and my legs, up to the knees, go numb. I keep walking. Waves cover me, crash into me. It feels good, like the craziness that is my world on the inside somehow comes alive out here on the outside.

"Are you okay?" Someone's voice comes over me.

I look up and see wide green eyes, tossed blonde hair, bleached in parts from the sun and the salt.

"Is everything okay?" he asks, his voice deep and concerned. "Sorry, I don't want to bother you, but you're just swimming in your clothes and I just wanted to make sure that you're all right."

I lift up my hand as the few rays of sun that peek through the clouds blind me. It's surprisingly dark outside, but still bright, leaving you in need of sunglasses. He extends his hand and I just take it. I'm not sure why, except that no one has asked me how I was doing for a really long time, and it feels nice to have someone care.

I hold his hand until we walk all the way back up to the beach, at which point I pull away.

"I'm Logan," he says.

"Kelly." I nod.

Now that I get a closer look at him, I doubt that he's even a day over twenty. There's innocence in his eyes, making me feel ancient even though I'm probably just five years older.

"I'm going to be fine," I say. "Just wanted to feel the water on me."

"Are you sure about that? Some people walk in there and have stones in their pockets, hoping the ocean will take their problems away."

"Does it work?" I ask, raising one eyebrow. Logan doesn't find that funny.

"I guess for some people, but it won't for you, not while I'm here."

It sounds more like a threat than a request for me not to commit suicide, and I can't help but laugh.

"I don't have any rocks," I say, pointing to the pockets on my dress. "See?" I pull them out and that seems to satisfy him.

"Okay, well, in that case, sorry to bother you." He leans on his surfboard, dressed in a wetsuit. I can see the firmness of his body. He's tall and wiry. His hair is blonde and long and falls slightly in his face.

"Have you ever been surfing?" he asks, positioning his board just so to cast a shadow over my face and to keep the sun out of my eyes.

"No, I haven't."

"Would you like to try? I mean, you're already halfway in. You don't seem to be bothered much by the cold."

I shrug. "Only because I've already gone numb, right? Well, maybe for a little bit."

"Here, let me show you."

We walk out into the waves where they break and then a little bit past that. He shows me how to climb onto the board and how to position my feet just so. It looks so easy when all of these seal-looking, wetsuit-clad guys do it.

They bop on their boards out in the ocean, but I struggle to even get on and stay on, let alone get up all the way to my feet.

Logan doesn't laugh. He doesn't poke fun. His patience is everlasting almost, endearing. He's the complete opposite of my ex-husband. He puts me at peace.

One time, I went to this New Age type of store that sold crystals. I've never been much of a believer, but I walked around and I took an amethyst in my hand, and just holding it, the coolness of the rock in my palm put me at ease immediately. I wish I could have bought it, a big one that I could really grab onto, but it was too expensive, not at all affordable.

Being here with Logan, him showing me how to ride the waves, his patience and the calmness of his voice and the complete lack of frustration with anything, it just puts me into that same relaxed state that I felt in that crystal store, and I want more and more of it.

When I begin to shiver, Logan cuts our lesson short and tells me that next time I need to bring a wetsuit.

"There's not going to be a next time," I say, getting out of the water. Holding onto my shoulders, I wrap myself in my regular bathroom towel. Luckily, I brought this for the trip.

"What are you talking about? You're a natural. You're going to be up in no time."

"No, I don't know, I don't think so," I say. "Wetsuits are expensive, boards are expensive, and this is not for me."

"I don't get that sense at all," he says, tossing his hair. "You love the water; that's why you're here. Even though it's cold and not all that inviting today, I saw that smile on your face when you got up on the board. People who surf, they do it because it becomes kind of a religion. You come out here to the water to worship your god, the natural world. I can feel that you understand what I'm getting at when I say that. Most people look at me like I'm crazy. But you feel the way I feel in the water, don't you?"

I swallow hard and take a step away from him.

"I have to go," I say, turning around to walk away.

"No, don't," he says.

He follows after me and I'm having trouble making much progress because the sand is choppy and my footing is unsteady. Luckily, the beach isn't very wide, and I get to the end quite quickly, but Logan catches up with me.

"I'm sorry, I didn't mean to scare you. I'm not a freak, I promise," he says. "I just feel this kind of intense feeling about you, like I know you. I know that's messed up and probably creeping you out. So I'll go now."

He turns to walk away, demanding nothing more from me, and the more steps that he takes, the more that the calmness I felt just a little bit ago, being next to him, starts to dissipate.

The anxiety that brought me here crawls back in, so I yell his name and catch up to him. Each step I take, the feeling of serenity and calmness returns, like this is the person that I should be near right now. I don't know about long-term or any of that stuff, but in this moment there's safety here.

"Thanks for showing me how to do that," I say, taking big pauses in between each word, trying to extend our time together and hold onto this feeling for as long as possible.

"Of course."

We stand right in front of each other and I wait for him to demand something more of me, but he doesn't. He just exists in the moment like I do, without pressure, without a rush.

"You hungry? Would you like to get something to eat?" Logan asks.

Another gust of wind comes. I'm leaning a little bit to the side, my footing unsteady, pushing me closer to him.

"Sure," I say. "I'd like that."

4

KELLY

It doesn't look like much from the outside but the food is delicious. It melts in your mouth and makes you feel like you're part of some secret society.

"They're always here," Logan says, giving me a wink. "It's a special spot for surfers."

"What are you trying to say exactly? That I'm a surfer? Yeah, right." I toss my head back and laugh.

"I saw you out there. You almost got on the board. That's how you start. It's never too late."

"Yeah, I'm not so sure about that," I say, watching him take another bite. He wipes his fingers, meticulously, with a napkin and then hands me a clean one. I take it and put it in my pocket while I hold up my plate and scarf down the burrito. The vegetables are so fresh. They taste like they have just come out of the earth.

I take another bite. Logan is all done with his, having inhaled it completely. He leans against the bench, spreading his legs out wide, and draping his arm slightly behind me. I feel the magnetic pull toward him, unexplainable, and difficult to pinpoint.

He asks me about my life and I gloss over some of the details. When I mention my son and my ex-husband, I feel ancient like I have lived this life that is well out of his reach.

"Tell me about you," I say, taking my time with the burrito, eating slower than I normally do just to have more time here, alone with him.

The salt on my skin and in my hair has dried, leaving a little residue. My hair's crunchy and moves slightly in the wind. When I lick my lips, they feel salty as well.

"I was in foster care for a long time, have a grandmother somewhere out in the desert, but she wanted nothing to do with me. My parents are on drugs. They were never meant to care for a child. I lived in ten homes before I stopped counting, managed to graduate from high school. Worked for a while at a surf shop, saved up enough money for a board and a wetsuit. The guy sold it to some conglomerate, a chain. They fired me."

"What do you do now?" I ask.

"I opened a surf school, online, charge for lessons, operate from the beach. I ask people to bring their own wetsuits and boards, or I let them use mine."

"How's that going?" I ask.

"Pretty good. Just moved out from my car into a studio apartment, got a better cell phone, paying my bills. I'm going to be expanding it into something bigger, going to buy new boards. Wet suits. Really trying to build it into something."

The more he talks, the more comfortable I get. We have a lot in common but I keep it to myself for now.

Keeping my past private has been a way for me to stay safe, to hold onto my privacy, to protect myself against those who might want to hurt me. Logan doesn't seem like someone who would do that, but then again, I didn't think that Sonny was capable of that either.

"Let me pay you for my lunch," I say, opening my wallet.

"No, absolutely not."

"Come on, please, don't be silly."

I reach for the couple of bucks that I have in there, but he leans over and just takes it from me and puts it back into my bag.

"It's my treat. I'm doing well. I can take a girl out on a date."

"No, this isn't a date," I say, shaking my head. "I can't."

I expect for the expression on his face, the smile to fall, but it doesn't; instead he looks mildly amused.

"Well, in that case, let's just call it a lunch between friends."

I get the feeling that he understands so much more of me than I could ever say out loud. And that's the feeling that scares me the most.

What is it that he gets?

What is it that he sees that I don't?

I MEET Logan again the following day. Mikey is with his father the whole weekend. So, I drive down to Oceanside once again to go surfing, or in my case, boogie boarding. I figure that if we are meant to find each other, we will once again, but he isn't there.

I stay for a couple of hours, coming in and out of the water, forcing myself to get a little bit more acclimated. I continue to struggle to withstand the temperature for long. Then just as I'm about to leave, Logan walks up to me: hair dry, long and tossed, bright white teeth, a nice golden brown tan wrapping all around his body.

"I'm just about to leave," I say. "I've been here for two hours."

"Oh, that's too bad. You should have called."

Logan had given me his number yesterday. I put it in my phone in a secret file under a calculator app. This is the way I kept secrets from my husband when we were still together.

He wasn't very technologically savvy, but he checked my phone all the time: the text messages, the e-mails. I had to give over all of my passwords. What Sonny didn't know was this app.

I never cheated on him. I was faithful even though he was anything but that. This is the way I talked to the few friends that I managed to make at school, and since the messages mainly focused on how abusive he was and them begging me to leave him and me finding reasons to stay, I couldn't have that anywhere near my regular messages.

I contemplated writing Logan last night, just a casual text, but hesitated and put the phone away. I need to be alone. I can't jump into another relationship, or romance, or whatever this is.

"Do you want to get lunch again?" he asks. "I meant to come out here earlier, but I had a private lesson in Huntington Beach. I couldn't turn it down. The money was too good."

"But you came here anyway?" I ask.

"Yeah, I had a feeling that maybe you'd be here. Wanted to see you."

He shifts his weight from one foot to another. Our eyes lock again.

Instead of that familiar feeling of comfort, I suddenly feel like I'm falling, no parachute, nothing holding me up. The only way to make the feeling go away is to look away from him.

I dry myself haphazardly with the towel and put on a sweater. I'll put my yoga pants on by the car once my legs dry a little more. Taking the boogie board, I head toward the parking lot.

"I have to go," I say, not so much to him, but past him somewhere in the distance.

"Did I do something wrong?" Logan asks.

"No, not at all. I just have a very complicated relationship with my ex. He has my son now, and I'm not looking for anyone or anything else to complicate my life. There isn't time for this, whatever *this* is. Besides, I'm too old for you."

Logan reaches for my hand and intertwines his fingers with mine. We still haven't kissed. I wonder if I had assumed too much. But I needed him to know.

"What about just friends?" he asks.

His hand doesn't let go of mine, and I hold him there, feeling the warmth emanating from it and letting it wrap all around me.

"I don't have time for friends," I say, looking back but not having the strength to actually pull my hand away.

Without letting go, Logan leans down and picks a little yellow flower from the side of the road.

"This is for you," he says. "Look at this, close your eyes, and make a wish and it's going to come true."

I shake my head no. Our fingers are still touching, but taking the flower is going to make this real, whatever the heck it is.

"What's wrong?" Logan leans down toward me, bending his knees slightly. Our eyes are now level.

"I don't want this," I say, waving my arm in between us.

That's a lie. I've never felt so comfortable and at peace in someone else's presence.

It's not just that he's the complete opposite of my ex-husband. It's more that he makes me feel so relaxed and yet he scares me, but in a good way, like maybe it's okay to be happy.

Maybe life can be more than just a struggle.

I don't know how he can make someone feel this way given where he came from and what he has been through. I want to find out, but because of this fear, I'm too scared to get closer.

He licks his lips and the lower one glistens in the sun.

"How about this?" Logan says with a casual shrug. "I'll hold onto this flower and to your wish, and you call me any time when you want to talk, and I'll be there for you, no matter what. No pressure."

"Just like that?" I ask.

"Yeah, just like that."

I hesitate for a moment and then take a step forward and kiss him.

5

As soon as we're alone, Luke takes me into his arms and kisses me on the mouth.

"I can't believe you're here," he says, his hands cradling my face. "I mean, you said you weren't coming."

Luke kisses me again and again and I hug him back tightly, knowing that I've made the right decision, that all the fear I had felt vanishes when I'm in his arms.

"Let me show you our room," he says, grabbing my hand and pulling me up the stairs to where he had put my bag when we first came in.

I pull away briefly and look at the family pictures gracing the whole stairwell to the second floor.

Luke and Sam and their brothers as teenagers with their parents laughing on a fishing trip. Little four-year-old Luke standing on the beach with his pail next to a sand castle that he had built. Surprisingly, yet perhaps not surprisingly, he looks exactly the same. Same eyes, same familiar grin.

"You look like you got older but I could still pick out the fact that you're this little kid." I laugh, pointing to the toothy smile.

"Yeah, I was pretty cute, huh?" he says, without missing a beat and I laugh. He grabs my hand and I follow him upstairs, trying to keep my laughter down.

His bedroom is located at the far end of the house and the floorboards creak as we walk. I rise up to my tiptoes and hold my breath.

"You know that they know we're adults and you're staying here with me, right? And that you're my girlfriend."

"I know. I still feel a little weird," I say with a little shrug. "I mean, this is your parents' house."

"Yes, but we're in our thirties. It would be weirder if we didn't sleep together."

He tilts his head to one side and crosses his arms. I chuckle and reach over, taking his hand in mine. There's a big window adorned with antique style drapery and a window seat underneath right next to the dresser.

Luke pulls me close to him. The floors are hardwood, recently polished and glistening in the warm candlelight. There's a faux candle in the corner next to the antique dresser and a nineteenth century style four poster bed.

I pull away briefly and tell him that I should unpack but he says that I can do it later. As I kneel down, he drapes his body over me and pulls me back. I turn around to kiss him and we end up on the bed.

The following morning, I wake up with Luke lightly snoring into his pillow facing the window. There's a bird jumping on a big branch outside. I rise, stretch out, do a few sun salutations, and look out the window at the prairie.

The place looks completely different from last night. Any creepiness or uneasiness I felt driving up to this old farmhouse has all but vanished. In fact, it feels incredibly cozy and comfortable to be here.

I hear Luke's family downstairs, giggling. The adults' laughter is pierced by the loud excitement of the baby. I put on a loose-fitting pullover and a pair of yoga pants and head downstairs in my socks, hair piled on top of my head.

Teddy laughs as Miranda tries to get him to eat something in his high chair. Sam is on his phone, and Bea and Ross are in the kitchen joking around while the TV, set to The Disney Channel, blares. As soon as they see me, they shower me with hugs and ask me about my night's sleep.

"The bed is really comfortable," I say.

"I'm glad to hear that." Bea nods, wiping her hands on her apron. "Miranda insisted on an older bed frame to match the character of the house, but I wasn't so sure."

"Well, it wasn't made out of straw."

"Yes, we did compromise on that, Miranda." Bea smiles. "The mattress had to be top-notch. I've had back problems my whole life and there was no way I was going to have my guests sleeping on something uncomfortable and not Tempur-Pedic."

"It was great. The best night's sleep in a long time, thank you."

"Did you see the remote next to it? The bed actually lifts up."

"Oh, no, I didn't, but it was great just the way it was. I really love the end tables. They look really authentic," I say, trying to think of something nice to say. It's not that it's not true; it's just that I tend not to care about interior decor all that much.

Bea smiles and thanks me along with Miranda. When Sam gets off the phone, he comes over and gives me a brotherly squeeze.

"Sorry, I was just busy with a client." The casualness with which this family expresses emotions and doles out affection takes me by surprise.

It has always been such a complicated and distant thing in my own family. Something that we saw people do on TV, but never did ourselves.

When Luke comes downstairs, he hugs everyone as well, and we sit down to have the French toast casserole that his mom has made. I grab a slice and top it with fresh, cut up strawberries and a few blueberries. A pot of black coffee makes its way around the lazy Susan in the middle of the dining room table and conversation shifts from pop culture to funny stories of their past and even talk of a new baby.

Miranda waves her arms in protest and so does Sam, but they do exchange a little smile that they think no one else sees and I wonder if they're keeping a secret.

The French toast is delicious and lathered generously in syrup and powdered sugar, giving me that much needed dose of dopamine. I'm a big sugar addict and it's something that I have struggled with for most of my life.

"So, tell me about your work," Ross says, directing the question to me.

I have briefly discussed a little bit about my personal life growing up in Big Bear and what that was like, avoiding the situation with my sister to not dampen the mood.

"LAPD detective is pretty impressive."

"Not exactly an FBI agent, but I'll take it. There are just different law enforcement agencies."

"Don't be so humble," Luke says, giving me a wink.

I tell them about graduating from USC and wanting to pursue a graduate degree.

"What made you think that was something that you wanted to do?" Bea asks.

"It's actually something that I've wanted to do for a long time. My father was killed," I say, the words just slipping out of my mouth.

Bea narrows her eyes and leans forward. I suddenly regret making this wonderful breakfast such a downer by bringing my dose of realism and darkness.

"Sorry, we don't have to talk about this."

"No, please do," Ross says.

"Yes, what happened?" Miranda shakes a rattle in Teddy's face to keep him occupied.

"When I was twenty, my dad was shot in the stomach and he passed away. My mom, and I guess the police, believed that it was a suicide, but I'm not convinced. After that happened, I was sort of thinking about going into law enforcement and after graduating college and working a few different jobs, I just decided to go for it. My mom was angry. She didn't think that law enforcement was the place for a girl, not just a girl, but me in particular. But I guess that's one of the reasons I decided to pursue this line of work."

"What happened with your father?" Ross asks.

"Well, I work for the LAPD, and I work lots of crazy hours and the whole thing was so traumatic, you'd think that I would pursue the case right away, but I didn't. To tell you the truth, I never even talked to anyone there about it. My mom could be right. It could have been suicide. He was somewhat depressed, but he struggled with that on and off his whole life. There wasn't anything particularly different about the situation."

I keep talking, my words running ahead of my thoughts, if that were possible. I don't know why I tell them all this stuff that I've never told anyone, but for some reason I just feel so at peace here, so comfortable.

A part of me feels like they could be the family I never had, and that if anyone were to understand, besides Luke, why I never pursued my father's case, then maybe it would be them. Of course, I know I'm projecting. I've met them once, and just because they gave me a general feeling of comfort doesn't mean that they aren't people with flaws and problems, and all the typical crap that accompanies humanity. But still, I tell them a lot. I tell them about my dad being a drug dealer and all the other things that I suspect.

"I just don't think that he could have killed himself," I say, watching as they hang on my every word, their eyes big like saucers staring at me. Luke puts his hand on my knee and gives it a light squeeze telling me that it's going to be okay, that it's fine for me to go on.

"He shot himself twice and he bled out for a long time. The problem is that the more time that passes, the more I think that I should have investigated it earlier and I never did, and I can't help but blame myself for it."

"Don't," Ross says, shaking his head. "That's a very natural feeling, but don't do it. You weren't ready to find out the truth yet. But now that you are, now that you can actually talk about it with us, you should pursue it."

I look over at Luke; he gives me a smile and suddenly, I feel like, of course, this is what I've been looking for.

I never thought I needed permission, but perhaps I did. Perhaps my mom's insistence that this was a stupid thing to pursue was exactly why I needed someone her age to tell me, Yes, you're ready to know the truth. You're ready to pursue it. You can do it. Whatever the truth is, you should find that out.

6

KELLY

On Sunday night at five p.m., I show up at my ex-husband's house. My heart drops as soon as I walk up to his door. I ring the doorbell and say a silent prayer that Sonny answers it. I hear lots of voices on the other side along with a booming early '90s soundtrack.

The plethora of Harley-Davidsons in the driveway tells me that they're having one of their regular Sunday dinners. Sonny's mother grew up on the east coast and the Italian Sunday dinner is a prerequisite in their family.

She cooks pounds of spaghetti and a whole bunch of other Italian food, and the dinner lasts from two in the afternoon until whenever. She loves being the hostess, the club mother. Her husband, Sonny's father, was the one who started this club, and as far as the general public is concerned, they do nothing but make a lot of noise and drive their Harleys in and out of this neighborhood late at night.

But what I know to be the truth is that the club runs on doing a protection racket for the Mexican cartel and they have a lot of connections in prison, enforcing laws and taking out witnesses who have anything to say against any members of the club or their affiliates.

They have also been expanding into running drugs and guns, doing small deals here and there for the cartel, but also expanding into their own business territory.

Much to my disappointment, Sonny is not the one who opens the door. It's Courtney. She's wearing a midriff top showing off her recently implanted double Ds. She has big Aqua Net hair with a tan to match. At one point, Courtney and I were friends, but then she started hooking up with my husband and things got, well, let's just say complicated.

"I'm here to pick up Mikey," I say, trying to remain as courteous as possible.

"Come on in," Courtney says, licking her lips demonstratively and popping a bubble with her gum. She waves her long acrylic nails as she waves me aside.

"Can you just please bring him out? Maybe ask Sonny to do that?"

"No, I won't. If you want Mikey, he's eating dinner with Grandma," she says, walking away from me, moving her hips from side to side like Shakira in her "Hips Don't Lie" video.

Courtney does have a beautiful body. She's at least five inches taller than I am and knows how to wear heels. Come to think of it, Sonny and I were never a good match. He's always wanted me to get breast implants and wear skimpier clothes so the others in the club knew how sexy I was. He wanted to show me off as a trophy, but I never wanted to be that kind of girl. My go-to outfit is a loose-fitting shirt, jeans, my hair up in a messy bun, with a little bit of makeup.

It was fine when we were in high school, but women in their early 20s, especially ones with nice bodies, like to show that off in LA, and I knew that the more tattoos he got, and the bigger that his motorcycle got, and the more money he had in his pocket from all those drug deals, the less he wanted to be seen with someone like me: plain Jane who'd rather stay in on a Friday night and read a book or watch some Netflix.

Come to think of it, I have no idea what the two of us were doing together at any point in our lives, except that there was a time when it felt like he could protect me from all the bad stuff that was happening.

I make my way through the crowded living room, bikers sprawled all over the place watching football, talking loudly, drinking beers, to find my four-year-old son at the table with a cigarette in his mouth, his grandmother laughing hysterically taking his picture.

"What is going on?" I snap. "Mikey!"

I pull the cigarette out of his mouth.

"It's not even lit," Dolores, Dee for short, says, her bangles dangling around her wrist. "This is just pretend, don't freak out, Kelly."

"I do not want my son touching a cigarette, let alone being photographed with one. There's nothing funny about smoking."

Dee gets up and takes a drag of her cigarette, which has been practically surgically implanted in her hand, and blows smoke into my face.

"You think you're going to get cancer from *this*? Please. You're going to get shot on the street before any of that happens, so who cares."

That's the kind of thinking that I don't want my son to be around. "Sonny?" I yell out for my ex. "Do you know what your mother was doing?"

Sonny comes out of the back bedroom, putting a tank top over his tattooed, muscled body. His hair is messed up and a girl I've never seen before follows him out, long shirt draped down to her knees. I glance over at Courtney with eyes narrowed from anger. We both know what he was doing back there with this new girl, but I'm not sure if he's trying to make me mad or her mad. I don't take the bait.

"I'm sorry, Mommy," Mikey says quietly.

"Don't you apologize for that." Dee curls her finger in his face.

"Don't tell him what to do; he's my child." I reach over, but stop short of touching Sonny's mother, my ex-mother-in-law.

Things like this get escalated fast and I need to maintain my composure and make the appropriate complaint to the appropriate body so that Mikey can be mine once and for all.

"What's the problem?" Sonny asks, taking a sip of his beer nonchalantly, not giving a crap about anything that's been going on.

I take a few steps closer to him, making sure that he can hear me over the loud speakers in the living room and all of the voices.

"You're supposed to take care of him on your weekends. You're not supposed to drop him off for her to take care of him."

"I live here," he says. "Who cares who's taking care of him?"

"The court. He's *your* responsibility. You wanted fifty-fifty custody. And now you're not even spending time with him, and you're letting your mother pose him with cigarettes like it's a joke."

"It is a joke," Dee snaps, lighting another one.

"Can we talk outside?" I ask, calmly taking Mikey by the hand and grabbing his backpack which, luckily, is already packed.

Sonny follows me out and his group of friends exclaim in our direction. It's that sound that kids make when someone gets called to the principal's office in elementary school.

"When you have custody," I say to Sonny on the porch, closing the door behind us. "I want you to spend time with Mikey, and not in this house with all of this stuff going on."

"You know, you never liked my family," he snaps. "This is why we didn't work out."

"No, we didn't work out because you cheated on me and you lied to me and you started running drugs," I say the last part under my breath. Despite everything, I know that my son has to spend time with this man and I can't bad-mouth his father in front of him.

“Oh, God!”

"You know, you think you're so high and mighty, but I know you're up to no good, too," he says, throwing his fingers in my face. "One of these days I'm going to find out what it is that you're up to and you're going to lose custody of him once and for all and that will be the end of it."

He glares at me, but I've heard these threats before. I let them wash over me. I don’t let them penetrate deep inside, where they turn into fear.

I need to get away from Sonny and this place and I feel like there's a ticking clock over my head.

But how? I need Mikey to be with me. I could never do this without him. I could never give him up to this family, to this terrible existence.

"For now, if you want to spend time with him, you spend time with him," I say, walking to the car. "Those pictures of him with that cigarette, that's not okay and you know it."

I get in the car, buckle Mikey into the car seat, and drive away without looking in the rearview mirror.

7

KELLY

Gripping the steering wheel, my heart pounds. Mikey smiles and sings “Baby Shark” over and over again. "Did you listen to that when you were at your grandma's?" I ask.

"No, she wouldn't let me.” He shakes his head.

"Why not?" I ask.

"She said it was for babies and I'm a big boy."

His words are still a little slurred. He was going to speech therapy, which I had been paying for exclusively, since insurance won't cover anything, but Sonny made me stop.

He and his mom decided that Mikey didn't need speech therapy any more, with all their vast education, and that even though Mikey was a bit behind, he was going to get caught up all on his own.

I can't think of how many times I've heard this kind of toxic reasoning from them. When he was three, I took him to Target and let him pick out his own shoes. They were bright pink. He loved them as soon as he saw them. Bright lights going on and off.

I offered the blue ones and the green ones with the same lights, but he was insistent on the pink ones, and so I got them for him.

Well, his father lost it. As soon as he saw them, he yelled at him and yelled at me and made him take them off. Sonny caused such a scene that a year and a half later, Mikey sometimes still brings it up and tells me how much he loved those shoes and wished he could wear them.

I wasn't sure what to do at first. That was still when we were together, me just at the beginning of trying to leave.

But I know that Mikey needs one parent in his life to be someone he can trust, a rock that he can turn to no matter what and no matter who he is. I know that pink shoes aren't going to turn him gay, as if clothing, or anything else for that matter, could do such a thing.

Just like not wearing pink clothes does not make you not gay.

But Sonny and his motorcycle club peddle so much toxic masculinity that shoes like that are somehow a threat to everything that they are.

How pathetic is that?

When we get home, I curl up in bed with Mikey and we read his favorite books about fire trucks, ambulances, and police officers. He loves cars so much. Cars, dinosaurs, and Peppa Pig, the last one became another little secret between me and Mikey, something that he now knows well enough not to ask his father to put on the TV.

I put Mikey to bed early because I doubt that anybody was abiding by the 8:00 bedtime at his father's house, let alone caring enough to put him down for a nap, or to keep the house quiet. At first he says he doesn't want to, but as I turn the lights down low and read to him in a quiet and low tone, his eyelids start to grow heavy and he starts to drift away into a peaceful sleep.

I watch Mikey sleep for a little bit, noting how he looks exactly like Sonny: same bone structure, same hair, same eyes. He's going to be a looker, handsome, confident. And I wonder what other aspects of his father he has inherited.

There was a kindness that Sonny had. I felt like he could protect me from anything. What I didn't know was that all these years later, I'd need to find protection *from* him, and that what happened in foster care, though tragic and awful, didn't even come close to the darkness that I've seen this motorcycle club put their members and their women through.

There are those who like to play ball, there are those who get off on the power, like Dee, and maybe Courtney, though I'm not so sure. But then there are others like me who they grind up and push out because we don't comply, because we dare to live life on the straight and narrow and we want to make money the honest way.

As I tiptoe out of Mikey's room, I look at my phone. I go to the living room, grab my iPad, and search for something to watch on Netflix. I have a big TV, but I feel more comfortable this way. It's more intimate somehow. My phone dings.

Can I see you? Logan texts.

I'm tempted to ignore it, but I feel that pull again, only this time I'm going to be smart about it. I don't know anything about Logan, and if I were to see him, I need to make sure that I know more.

Yes, under one condition, I text back.

Anything.

Give me your full name, a copy of your driver's license, and your Social Security card.

He doesn't ask me why; he just screenshots it all and sends it. Probably not a wise move if I'm someone whose plan is to steal his identity, but I'm not. I just need to find out who he really is.

I sign up for the most expensive background search service available online. This is usually reserved for private investigators, but I don't have enough money to pay someone like that, so I do the research on my own. I put in his Social Security number, his full name, his driver's license number, and the records start to come up.

There is mention of a foster care home but no specifics and no juvenile hall records. They are sealed, but something would show up if there was a case number available. In this case there isn't.

I do find the name of his social worker, but nothing else, not even a parking ticket, let alone an arrest.

The following morning, I call the social worker and I ask her about him. She's surprised to hear from me, so I briefly mention that I have a history of being in foster care and I want to know everything about Logan before we get any closer as friends or anything else.

That somehow clicks.

"Yes, of course," she says, looking through her files. "I understand that you have to be careful, especially if you have a child."

I swallow hard. I didn't tell her this, but I guess she suspects.

"From my records, he's a very nice guy. Easy-going. I had a few meetings with him. He played with my daughter. No arrest record. A lot of homes, but no abuse allegations."

"From him, or from others on him?" I ask.

"Either. Certain things didn't work out. He had some bad luck, but not as bad luck as some kids end up having."

I know what she means. We're all dancing around the topic.

"Would you trust him with your child?" I ask.

"One hundred percent," she says. "And I wouldn't lie to you. I don't get calls like this very often, though more people should call to verify."

After I hang up, I let out a sigh of relief. I pick up my phone and I text Logan to see if he wants to meet me for lunch while Mikey is in preschool.

Of course. When? Where? He texts back.

8

I stay in Wichita for a couple of days and Luke shows me around. We drive out to the old development where he grew up, a cul-de-sac where a little boy and girl ride their bikes around their driveway. He then takes me to his old high school, a large sprawling suburban school, that had more than four hundred kids in his graduating class. The building is rather nondescript, wide and tall, no grand entrance out front like the kind that older schools used to have.

"The biggest problem with this place was that there weren't enough windows," he says with a sigh. "There's this whole interior part with the hallways inside and a lot of my classes had no natural light at all. So, I'd get on the bus for an hour in the dark, get home on the bus when it was dark. And during school hours, I'd never see the light of day."

"Not even during PE?" I ask.

"Oh, you mean gym? No, they had it indoors because, you know, the weather sucks but still, you need to get outside sometime, right? I hated growing up here," he says, looking at me. "I mean, I had my group of friends, but in general I just couldn't get away fast enough."

"And now?" I ask as we sit in the parking lot looking at the school out in the distance.

"Now it feels a little different. I mean, I still probably don't want to move back here, though I miss my family a lot, but I kind of see why we lived here. It was a good area. It wasn't a private school, so it was actually affordable. My parents did their best."

"Yeah." I nod. "I really like them, you know? They're so fun and easygoing. I'm sorry that my mom is not exactly like that."

"No problem," he says with a casual shrug.

"You're used to dealing with crazy people, right? Because you're an FBI agent," I joke.

He gives me a coy smile, brushing his fingers through his hair. "Have you given any more thought to what we talked about before?"

"You mean, moving in? I like it." I laugh.

"Anything else?"

"Yeah, I can see marrying you," I say, my face suddenly getting serious. "Why? Are you proposing?"

"Well, definitely not here. Not like this."

"You're going to make me wait for it?" I sit back in the rental car, surprised. Taking a sip of his latte, he winks at me.

"Of course you're going to have to wait for it. It's our engagement. It's going to be a whole thing."

"A whole thing? No, no, no, no," I say quickly. "I do not want to make a big deal out of it."

"Okay. Let me ask you something then."

I turn to face him, sucking down a bit of the Starbucks pink drink and letting the explosion of flavors wash over me.

"When have you ever wanted something to be made a big deal?"

I tilt my head to one side and peer into his eyes. "I'm just not that kind of girl."

"You don't want a big wedding?"

"I don't know, I never thought about it."

"Of course, you have. What about Sydney?"

"What about her?" I ask.

"She's getting married. You're going to be doing the whole bridal shower thing; you're going to be the bridesmaid. You already helped her pick out the dress and you know exactly how that went."

“I mean, who wants to be a part of that?” I shrug.

“It's because her family is crazy, but it doesn't have to be that way."

"I kind of feel like it does," I say slowly. “But you want a big wedding, don't you?" I add.

He looks up at me.

"I wouldn't say that exactly, but I want my family to be there. I want to make the commitment to you. Is that so wrong?"

"It's expensive."

"Let's not do it expensive. I can't believe that we're talking about this. I mean, what if you're a terrible roommate?"

"Well, then I can become your stay-at-home husband and take care of everything."

"That's the second time you mentioned that," I say. "Quitting your job."

He looks away from me and toward the big, imposing, windowless building looming above the plains before us. The grayness of the weather is not adding to the overall mood of the moment.

"Yeah, I've been thinking about it quite a lot," Luke says, looking out into the distance. “I'm just not happy with the work schedule. It's not really for me, the hours, the unpredictability, I want to do something else."

I nod.

"The only really good thing about it is the retirement, but I honestly don't know if I'll make it that far. You have to live in the now, right? In the present."

“So, let me get this straight," I say, finishing the rest of my drink and dropping it into the cupholder. "You just want to marry me and then what? Give up your job and have me take care of you forever?"

"Hmm, that does sound rather appealing," he jokes.

I lean over and kiss him. “Well, I want you to be happy."

"Really?" he asks.

"Yeah. I want you to find something that you love doing and pursue that." He kisses me back.

When we pull away from the school, my phone rings. It's Captain Medvil.

"I'm off, right?" I say, showing the screen to Luke.

He shrugs. "You are, but you know how this job is. You're not really off."

"Should I answer it?"

"Up to you."

"You need to come back here," Captain Medvil says, without bothering with hello.

"Why? What happened?"

"A body has been found in the LA River."

9

"I know that you have plans for your days off, but you need to come back early," Captain Medvil says.

I'm about to ask why, but he continues.

"Abrams and Martel are currently on leave, and everyone else's caseloads are out of control. Is there any way you can come back?"

"Why is Abrams on leave?"

"There was an incident."

"What kind of incident?" I press.

"Somebody recorded him placing this kid under arrest. Kid said something to him while he was on a gurney heading to the ambulance; he had been shot.

Abrams turned around and punched him in the face and he's in a coma."

My mouth nearly drops open.

"Yeah, okay. I'll be there as fast as I can. I'll try to get a flight later today, tomorrow morning at the latest."

"We'll be dealing with this crime scene for a while. I'll text you the address. Come straight from the airport."

On the drive over to Olive Garden where we're meeting with Luke's family, I fill him in on what the captain has just said.

"Holy crap, so Thomas just attacked him?"

"Yeah, luckily some bystander caught it on video and posted it on Twitter."

"This might be a way to get him off the force." Luke smiles and I feel the corners of my mouth going upward as well.

It's not that I'm happy that this poor kid got attacked and is now in a coma, I'm just glad that there's finally a record of who Thomas really is.

"So, he was tied to a gurney?"

I search for the video on Twitter and it doesn't take me long to find it.

LAPD Officer Punches an Injured Suspect While on a Gurney, one of the headlines reads. I play it, and there it is.

Thomas walking away, a kid, fifteen or sixteen years old, yelling a curse word in his direction.

Thomas returning and punching him three times squarely in the nose.

The thing about attacks like this is that you never know how someone might react.

I've seen a number of one-punch homicide cases where a drunk bar patron throws his fist in the wrong guy's face. That guy passes out and dies and the guy who hit him gets sentenced to prison. In this particular case, however, someone finally caught Thomas's short fuse on camera.

I've seen him blow up like that a number of times. He did it to me, he did it to Catherine, and then he did it to numerous other people out there on the street that he's supposed to serve and protect. It doesn't matter if they had violated the law.

I'm not one of those cops who believes that everyone deserves a badge and a gun, and that we have to stand behind a thin blue line to protect them all. I feel like there're a lot of rotten apples and those rotten apples reflect badly on all of us good ones who do the right thing, show up and try to uphold the law without shortcuts, without letting our anger and tempers get in the way.

Luke knows about what has gone on between Thomas and me and he gives me a supportive squeeze of the hand as we pull into the parking lot. I see his parents, Sam, Miranda, and Teddy gather in the lobby through the window. They laugh and smile and the warm glow of the place wraps itself around them in that nice, sweet way, giving me a cozy, comfortable feeling of a place where I belong.

"I'm not going to say anything to them if you don't want me to," Luke says.

"Yeah, let's enjoy tonight. I have to get a ticket to get back to deal with this case, but I want to have a good time tonight."

"I'm glad you like my family," Luke says. "They like you a lot, too, probably a little bit better than they like me."

He laughs and reaches over and gives me a peck on the lips.

I like how comfortable we are with one another and how I finally feel like there's somebody who I can talk to about things that are going on with me.

It's not a feeling that I've had in a long time, being out there all on my own. I follow Luke inside, our fingers intertwined holding on tightly, and just at that moment I realize: this is *it* for me.

This is the man who I want to be with for the rest of my life.

10

I arrive at LAX at five in the morning and head straight to the address along the LA River that the captain texted me.

The Los Angeles River is a major river in Los Angeles County. Its headwaters are up in Simi Hills and it flows for over fifty miles through the San Fernando Valley, downtown LA, and down to Long Beach. It was once free-flowing and it frequently flooded, forming alluvial flood plains along its banks.

It's currently best known for the concrete channels that form a fixed course for it to flow through after a series of disastrous floods in the early 20th century. The LA River used to be the primary source of fresh water for the city, but it became heavily polluted with a lot of urban and agricultural runoff. The concrete channels that were built limit the absorption of the water into the earth, making the water flow fast even in the dry summer months.

The body was found under the freeway overpass on one of these concrete banks of the river. Crime scene tape has been put up, vans and police vehicles are set up for crime scene collection.

I meet with Sergeant Deaver and he mentions that a homeless person had called it in after finding the body in the afternoon. They camp out right around here.

The victim's hair was clean, so were her teeth. Just a little bit of dirt under the fingernails, which I hope can provide us with some information. Sergeant Deaver walks me through the crime scene, which has been secured. The homeless encampment here not as big as some others around the city, but the man who called it in had a shopping cart and a tent set up not far away.

"His friends were looking out for his stuff while he went to apply for a job," Sergeant Deaver says. "He was working with a social worker who confirmed this."

"So, this has nothing to do with the homeless population here?" I ask.

"I'm not sure, but she didn't seem like she lived on the streets. Unless this was her first night out."

I walk over to where the body was found, which had already been taken to the morgue. The crime scene is still set up and he shows me the photographs just as the sun is rising over the horizon. The victim's hair was blown out, she was dressed in a suit and heels. She's around twenty-five years old.

"What was she doing here?" I ask.

It's a rhetorical question, that's the whole point of my job. Sergeant Deaver gives me a moment to walk around and take in the location of the body. I look around the underpass, and there are a few tents about a hundred yards away, but according to Deaver everyone swears that the body was not there yesterday.

"Did someone pull over and throw it down here?" I ask. "Were there any abrasions on her from rolling down the concrete embankment?"

"Not that I could see, but the medical examiner will let you know," Deaver says, walking around, nursing a mug of coffee.

I can see a little bit of steam escape from the top, and the cold chill makes me pop the collar of my jacket and regret the fact that I left my warmer coat in the car.

Sometimes, when you don't get enough sleep, you tend to get colder. The cold seems to creep up on you, even in LA where the temperature is pretty moderate year-round.

Rush hour traffic makes cars inch above the overpass, with many of the drivers and passengers looking out at what we're doing down here. I hear the blades of a local news helicopter up above our heads, reporting on the scene, which is exactly why a tent has been set up to secure the area from prying eyes.

"But she hadn't been tossed down the embankment. Someone had to come down here and physically pull the body down."

“She didn’t seem like she had many abrasions,” Deaver points out.

“What if it were two people?” I ask.

"Perhaps," he agrees.

Deaver has a protruding belly and a receding hairline. He is in his fifties and has a friendly demeanor and a very nice second wife whom I’d met at the company picnic last summer.

She's a painter, if you can believe that, and teaches art at the University of Southern California.

Deaver and I have never had much of a friendly relationship, but a successful professional one. I've never even been out with him once at a bar with other cops because he had a new baby a few years back and spent all of his non-working time at home.

I guess he had learned something from what went wrong in his first marriage. From others, I've heard that he used to be a big drinker and partier who didn't care much for wedding vows and spent all of his overtime pay at the strip club.

It's amazing how people can change in the matter of a few years, and yet it's also amazing how others never change their whole lives.

I walk over to the homeless encampment and introduce myself. Even though it's only five a.m., everyone is awake and have been for hours.

They're not the kind of people that feel comfortable with police being right there, but luckily many of them stay around and were available to talk to us.

"We already answered all of that guy's questions," an annoyed older woman says, peeping out of her tent. "When is it going to be enough?"

"I'm sorry, ma'am, I just got here. Can I get your name?"

"You can call me Melissa," she says, not offering a last name.

I know that she probably goes by something else out here on the streets so that she can be easily identified, but she doesn't share that with me. I have no way of getting in touch with her because she has no phone, but I hand her my card, as I do with everyone else.

I ask everyone questions and they repeat almost the same thing that Deaver told me. The body was not here earlier in the day, and the first person to spot her was Frank, an older man who walks with a cane but likes to exercise his limbs every day in the afternoons by walking along the banks of the river.

Along this part, the river is just a few puddles and a lot of shrubbery growing along the concrete banks.

"I saw Frank walk out there. I thought it was a bag or something that someone had dropped. But then he was hurrying back and he had this crazy look in the eyes," Melissa says. "And I just knew something was wrong. We all walked out there and saw the body. She was lying face down. We didn't touch her; we didn't move her at all."

"Was she dressed in that suit?"

"Yes."

"Not wrapped in anything?"

"No, but you could tell she had been shot in the back of her head, red blood on blonde hair and all that."

I nod.

"So, we told him that he had to call it in since he was the one who spotted her. He didn't want to do it but he did. When the social worker came he told her, then they called the cops together. He used her phone to call you all."

The story checks out but the mystery remains. Who is this woman?

I walk away, looking at the crime scene photos that Deaver handed me in a packet. The story checks out, I probably won't need to interview Frank but I might. Luckily, the social worker has his information and a way to contact him.

I have some answers but not others.

Who is this woman? I look at her face in the crime scene photos; she's so beautiful and young dressed in this suit, probably going to a job interview, going to her job somewhere.

Who dropped her off here and why? One thing is for sure, she has no abrasions from rolling down the embankment. So, someone had carried her down here, perhaps even two people.

Then what? Did they just place her there and walk away? There were all these tents just right over there, they must have thought that someone would spot them. Or maybe they knew that they wouldn't. Maybe they knew that during the day there's only one person who watches everyone's stuff and everybody else goes along their way.

Maybe they knew that in a homeless encampment, daytime is like nighttime for everyone else. That's when they feel safe leaving their stuff and doing something while somebody trustworthy stays behind to keep guard.

Who could have done this to her? And why?

11

I go to talk to Dr. Laura Berinsky, the medical examiner, later that afternoon. We've been friends for a while and she recently had a baby.

Laura waves to me through the camera when I come on the intercom and she tells me that she'll be out in a few minutes. I wait in the antiseptic hallway, checking my emails as I sit on one of those flimsy plastic chairs. A few minutes later, Laura comes out, dressed in scrubs, and tosses her gloves into the trash can.

"What do you think?" I ask.

"No tattoos, no identifying marks of any kind, no abrasions. Didn't find any identification."

"We didn't find her wallet or phone either," I say.

"That's not good."

"Her face is pretty much intact since the bullet traveled down the back of her neck."

"So, there were no abrasions or cuts anywhere?" I ask. "Is there any way that someone could have tossed her body from the car?"

"I guess she could have fallen that way, but it seems very unlikely. She doesn't have any bruises at all. She had even cleaned out her pores on the bridge of her nose recently, either by going to a spa or using one of those strips. This girl is very well taken care of. Somebody will be looking for her," Laura says, giving me a sympathetic look.

"It's not that we don't take all cases seriously. There're just certain ones that really pull at our heart strings. Someone like this, with their whole life ahead of them."

"The good news is that you will probably be able to find out who she is soon, unless she's not from this area. Women like this have family members, boyfriends, sisters, mothers, children."

"Children?" I ask.

"Yeah, she had a C-section. By the scar tissue, it looks like it was maybe three to five years ago."

"So, she's a mother," I say.

"Yes."

"Any chance that she overdosed or was on drugs?" I ask.

"No, the toxicology report came back negative for all major narcotics. She was completely clean. No alcohol, no marijuana, no sleeping pills, nothing."

"The way that she was shot, it's an execution-style killing," I say, thinking out loud.

"Yeah, one bullet to the back of the head. The guy was leaning over her. She seemed to have been on her knees."

"She was?" I ask.

"Her pants were a little bit dirty around the knees. I took samples, not sure if we'll be able to find anything to connect the dirt to wherever it came from, but she was not killed there, just dumped."

"So, she was on her knees when she was shot?"

"The bullet traveled in a downward trajectory. It likely came from a .22 caliber, something small."

"Any likelihood that she was involved in anything illegal?" I ask. "Maybe the sex trade?"

Laura shifts her weight from one foot to another.

"Hard to tell. She could have been a very high-end escort if she were involved in anything like that. No bruises anywhere on her body, no sexual trauma of any kind. She was wearing a ring around her ring finger, so she might've been married. There's a little tan line there, but that's all I've noticed. We didn't find the ring. She might've stopped wearing it recently or perhaps she is married and someone took it off."

We walk back toward the body in the room, and I notice how clean the victim's hair looks, given what happened to her. There's just a little bit of dust, but it was definitely styled relatively recently. Her skin is perfectly white, with just tinges of blue and green.

I thank Laura for her time and walk out lost in thought.

Who could this woman be? What could have happened?

In situations where we don't find any identification and we need to identify the body, we refer to her as Jane Doe.

When I get back to my desk, I get in touch with my contacts at the local press, NBC, ABC, and CBS affiliates and their local TV stations and send out a picture and a description of our Jane Doe.

Chandra Beverley, a reporter with KTLA, is the first one to call me back and ask me questions about the body that we have found. I give her all the details except for the fact that she was shot execution-style. I just mention that it is likely a homicide. She takes careful notes and then asks if I'm willing to go on the news.

I say yes, even though I'm a bit nervous about it. This won't be my first time, but I'm not great at speaking in public. However, I have to do everything in my power to spread awareness.

We make the appointment. Chandra comes by with a cameraman an hour and a half later, and I record a short segment, going over all the details that we have found.

At this point, I've confirmed what we are and aren't telling the news media with Captain Medvil, and we decide to keep the gunshot wound and the execution-style killing, the manner of death, a secret. The interview goes well, and Chandra is pleased with the segment. She wishes me luck in finding out her identity.

I just hope that the press conference is enough to get us some leads.

12

When the report airs on the nightly news, we get a number of calls about sightings and everything else. It's not particularly unexpected since that's what happens when we have an attractive victim. It's a known certainty that the prettier that the victim is, especially if she is young, female, and white, the higher the ratings are and the more the news stations are interested in reporting on the disappearance.

We have people at the department going through the calls to see which ones are worth taking note of. But until we have Jane Doe identified, it's going to be hard to see which of these calls present relevant information and which don't.

"Detective Carr." A young female deputy with over ten years at the department waves me over. Diedra and I have been somewhat friendly at work, but not particularly close.

"There's one call here from a guy that says he knows her."

"Really?" I ask.

Diedra nods her head. "Yeah, he was certain. He said he went out with her a few times. He said they met at a beach in Oceanside."

"Oh, okay. Give me his number."

She fills me in a little bit, and then I take the call to my desk.

Logan Jemison answers on the first ring. His speech pattern is a little slow and nasally, the kind of accent that Southern California is known for, laid back surfer dude.

"I got a message that you called, Logan, about the woman that we found?"

"Yeah, she's dead?" he asks, somewhat out of breath.

"Well, yes, we found this body. It's her. She looks exactly like that."

"Oh my God, poor Kelly. What could have happened to her?"

When I ask Logan if he's willing to stop by the station, he says that he can, and shows up on time an hour later. He's dressed in a pair of loose-fitting tattered jeans that hang low off his hip bones and a worn, well-loved t-shirt. He has a very strong physique, tight muscles, and I'm not surprised when he tells me that he runs a surf school. His skin is tan and his hair has a streak of blond.

My desk area is busy and I want somewhere private to talk. I lead him to room nine, which is the most relaxed of the interrogation rooms with a couch, coffee table, and an IKEA floor lamp.

I sit him down and ask, "Can I get you anything? Coffee, soda?"

"No, I don't drink soda," he says dismissively. "I'll take a coffee though." He sits down on the couch, leans forward, and lets his head drop between his shoulder blades. His hair falls in his face.

He looks so young, I doubt that he's over twenty.

"Can you tell me a little bit about yourself?" I ask.

Logan swallows hard. "I really thought that Kelly and I had something."

When he looks up at me, I can see that his bright green eyes are filling with tears.

"She's just someone that I met that I really connected with, you know? It's so hard to explain. I don't meet a lot of people who really make you feel like that about the world."

"How old are you, Logan?" I ask.

"Nineteen, but I've been around."

"What does that mean?" I sit down on the couch next to him and take a sip of my coffee.

I'm not wearing a suit jacket, just a nice pair of slacks and a t-shirt. I want to look relaxed and open and that will hopefully get him to trust me more.

"I grew up in foster care," he starts.

I ASK Logan a little bit about his life. He tells me that he grew up in many homes, no real connection with his mother or father.

"I'm used to being on my own," Logan continues. "I've met a few girls here and there, but no one I really connected with. I have some friends, but Kelly, you know there're sometimes people who come into your life and they just ... things change. You feel a connection like you never did before. You feel like there's somebody walking the earth who could possibly understand what you're going through. I didn't feel that until I met her."

"How did you meet?" I ask.

"It was just a regular day at the beach. I shot the breeze with a few people, made some jokes, but nothing serious was supposed to happen. Then I saw her. There was this magnetic force pulling me close to her. We started talking. I didn't want to leave. I didn't want to stop. We had so much in common, even though on the surface, we had nothing in common at all. She was older than me. She had been married. She has an ex-husband. She has a child."

He keeps oscillating between talking about her in past and present tense.

"Did you meet this child?" I ask.

"No, Mikey was asleep the few times I came over. She made sure to check my background before inviting me. She checked if I had a criminal record. I don't have one, but she wouldn't let me step foot in her house without that. I was there when Mikey was asleep and we just hung out. Nothing happened. Well, except I kissed her just a little bit. But she told me that she wanted to take it slow. So we did."

"And you never slept together?" I ask.

"No. We were going to have another date, but then I didn't hear from her. I texted her and nothing. I thought something was wrong. I thought that there were some issues she was having with her ex-husband."

"Can you tell me more about that?" I ask.

"Kelly talked about him a little bit. She said they had a very complicated relationship. He wanted more time with their son. He didn't want them to get divorced. He was making life very hard for her. But he was abusive and she wanted to get away from that whole culture."

"Culture?" I ask.

"He is in a motorcycle club, The Nighthawks."

"Do you know if he was involved with anything illegal?"

"No. She didn't want to tell me too much. She wanted to talk about something good or light, something we could have fun with. Movies, books. We talked a lot. We talked about a lot of things. She was reading Schopenhauer and all of these other philosophers. She wanted to take psychology classes. She wanted to help little kids deal with their problematic childhoods."

"Can you tell me the last time you saw her?" I ask.

"It was Tuesday, the nineteenth, around two in the afternoon. She dropped Mikey off at preschool and we spent the day together. We went surfing and then she had to go and pick up her son. Actually, I think it was around one because it was a bit of a drive."

"Pick up from where?"

"He started going to preschool. He was there all day."

"Do you know if she worked anymore?"

"She was a nurse, but she was working part time and she was getting her application ready for a master's degree."

"In child psychology?" I ask.

He nods.

"Another thing that her husband criticized her about. He thought that psychology was crap. Stupid. No one with a strong enough personality needed it. But from what I understand, he was the one who needed psychology and a psychologist the most to deal with all the toxic crap that he had in his life. And then he put it on her and their child."

"Relationships are complicated," I say. "It may seem like they're cut and dry and there's someone who's right and someone who's wrong, but that's rarely the case."

"I know that," he says, nodding his head. "Of course, I know that. I was getting one side of the story, but it was a pretty compelling one. I think when you meet him, you'll understand."

13

Afterward, I take down Logan's information and hand him my card. He tells me that Kelly's last name is Flynn and she lives in a one bedroom apartment in Culver City, not too far away from the hospital where she works.

I talk to Luke briefly on the phone, check in with him, and he tells me that he's flying back tomorrow.

I head to Kelly's place, knock on all the doors for her neighbors, and talk to a few. There seems to be a consensus. She was a very nice woman, her little boy was friendly and sweet and they never really heard him. She'd just moved in a couple of months ago and they never heard her arguing with anyone or having any domestic issues whatsoever. The apartment building is a mixed-age place with young professionals, families, and a few retirees that have been there for years.

After talking to the neighbors, I head to her ex-husband's place, which is another residential neighborhood about half an hour away. It's a one story house, looks to be about fifteen hundred square feet from the outside, and a garage out in the backyard. A woman in her fifties with big hair, long nails, and pounds of makeup answers with an attitude. Her guard is already up as soon as she hears that I'm with the police.

"I don't know why you all come around here every time that something bad happens. This club can't be responsible for every crime in Los Angeles, can it?" she says, throwing her hair back.

She's wearing a push-up bra and has a nice body that she knows how to use with curves that she knows how to accentuate.

Her response to me after me simply stating my name takes me by surprise. Perhaps it shouldn't. The club is one of the most notorious motorcycle gangs in the city. It's only natural for cops to come around asking questions when we find unsolved crimes and murders that look like they might be involved.

But I'm not here to start a fight.

"I'm here to talk to your son, Sonny," I say. "Is he around?"

"Yeah, he's around, working on his damn chopper out back."

"What is this about?" she asks, lighting a cigarette.

She follows me as I walk down the driveway toward the garage. The backyard has a swing set and piles of trash and salvage to one side. They're probably not your ideal neighbors, but they're probably not someone you'd complain about either.

I find Sonny hunched over his motorcycle. I don't know much about bikes, but this one has a lot of chrome on it and it's as big as a La-Z-Boy recliner. AC/DC is blasting from the speakers, and, at first, he can't hear me over the music.

"I need to talk to you," I say, motioning to turn down the radio.

He takes a moment, looks me up and down, and then slowly moves over and turns down the music on his phone. But instead of pushing the button to just stop it, he lowers the volume one beat at a time.

"I need to talk to you about something important," I say. "It's concerning your ex-wife."

"What has she done now?" he says, putting his hands across his chest. He's wearing a tight tank top that makes his muscles protrude. He's fit and is not a stranger to the weightlifting bench. His arms are covered in tattoos, and he has a confident smirk on his face, like someone who has a little bit too much power.

14

Sonny sits down on a metal stool and glares up at me. He's challenging me with his eyes.

"When was the last time you saw your ex-wife?"

"She never picked up my son from preschool," he says.

"That didn't answer my question. When was the last time that you saw her?"

"I don't know. What does this have to do with anything? Why are you even here?"

I realize that my little game is probably not going to work. "I have some bad news for you, sir. We have found a body and I would like you to come in to identify it."

"What?" He leans forward. "What are you talking about?"

His mom peeks over my shoulder.

"Did something happen to Kelly?"

He looks genuinely surprised, but this could all be an act.

"Will you come in and identify it?" I show Sonny pictures and the expression on his face changes. He looks forlorn.

This isn't usually what we would do for the next of kin. But given the fact that they got divorced, he isn't really the next of kin of anymore, and his child is too young to make any identifications about his mother.

"Shit," he says, shaking his head. "It's her… fucking Kelly."

He buries his head in his hands.

"How could you do this? How could you just say it like that?" his mother yells at me and then runs over to her son.

Sonny begins to weep. When he looks up at me, tears run down his cheeks and I hesitate. I was certain that I didn't have much to go on, but the complicated divorce and the custody battle made him a good candidate.

Now, seeing those tears, I start to have doubts. He follows me on his bike over to the medical examiner's office so that we do the identification. Her body is under a sheet on the table. As soon as Sonny sees Kelly's face, he rushes over, tries to touch her, and I have to physically restrain him.

"Please do not touch the body," I repeat over and over again.

"The body? This isn't a fucking body. This is Kelly, my wife!" he yells into my ear, but lets me pull him back.

The sadness is genuine and I feel it. Tears flow down his cheeks and his arms collapse, shoulder blades protruding through his shirt. When he follows me out to the hallway, he slams his fist against the wall. Luckily not too hard, but clearly out of frustration.

About ten minutes later, when he's more composed, I take him to the same comfortable interrogation room, where I had just talked to Logan. The cameras are set up, Captain Medvil and others are watching through the feed on the other end.

"Can you tell me a little bit more about your relationship?" I ask. I'd handed him a can of Coke, but he's yet to open it. He just holds it in his hand and rubs his finger over the top.

"We met in high school. She had a really bad home life. Lots of foster care. Lived with different families. They didn't treat her well. Had to actually punch one of the dads. We started seeing each other in ninth grade and then she started telling me more and more about her life. She came in one day with a black eye, tried to lie about what happened. Finally admitted to me that her dad, her foster dad, did it to her that morning, but she couldn't miss school because she'd already had too many absences. I left on my lunch break and I broke his leg."

"You broke his leg? Did anything happen with that?"

"What do you mean?"

"Legally speaking?" I clarify.

"No, he didn't dare press charges. He knew who I was, but he kicked her out that night. So she came to live with me."

"At your house?" I ask.

"Yeah, my mom's house. Everyone stays here who is having any trouble with anything. It's kind of an open door policy."

"And how was your relationship after that?"

"It was great. She went to Cal State. We were all there when she graduated. We got married when she was in college. I didn't cheat on her…for a while."

I narrowed my eyes.

"I know what you think. That I'm a dick for even doing that. But you don't know what it's like to grow up in a motorcycle club where women are property. It's horrible, but it was just expected, especially given who my father was. I wasn't respected if I didn't fool around on my old lady, and of course, I wanted their respect. I was going to take over one day and I needed them to know that I'm like them."

"So, that's why you cheated on your wife?"

"That and things were more complicated with her. She didn't think like me anymore. We had a lot in common initially. We like the same music, like to drink. And then she stopped and she got busy with her job and she was hanging out with all these doctors. And I just felt like she was moving away from me. Like she was starting this whole other life that I wasn't a part of. I wanted to be more than anything. I loved her. We were drifting apart and opportunities came up. Real hot girls, two of them came onto me and I was already really drunk."

He hesitates for a moment and then puts his head in his hands.

"What happened then?" I ask.

"My friends recorded the whole thing and eventually the tape made it to her and she just couldn't deal with it. We fought all the time. And after a while, nothing was the same."

Sonny shakes his head and finally pops the can open and takes a few big gulps. I watch him. He bites his lower lip and then the inside of his cheek. He looks around and I see tears gathering in his eyes.

He tries to keep them at bay and at first he's successful. When they finally overwhelm him, he raises up his wrist and wipes his eyes.

"Sorry, I have allergies," Sonny says, trying to be the big brave man as if showing emotion makes you any less masculine.

“So, can you tell me what happened after?" I ask. "What was your relationship after you broke up?"

"It wasn't great. We had all sorts of problems about sharing custody of Mikey. She didn’t want him around my family, and she knows that my family is non-negotiable. It's the same family that took care of her when she needed it and she had no problem with how violent or scary they were when she needed protection."

I nod, telling him that I understand.

"Look, I'm not going to say that everyone has to understand how we live or what we do, but we're a brotherhood. We're family. We're there for each other.

We don't have that much out there in the real world. Everyone's out for themselves. And Kelly liked that at first. She loved it, in fact. She told me that things were complicated. She didn't think that this place was healthy or good. So, we went to court. She was supposed to keep certain things secret and she didn't."

"What does that mean?" I ask.

"She was making threats."

"About telling the authorities something about the club."

Finally, a little bit of a motive shows up. He flashes his eyes to meet mine.

"It's not what you think. She would never say a word. And this club, this has nothing to do with her murder."

"Are you sure about that? Maybe she made a lot of threats against people who weren't so enamored with her like you were."

"They would never do that. She was my ex-wife. She was the mother of my child. They know that I'd never forgive them."

"Doesn't mean that they wouldn't want to protect themselves. What was she going to talk about? What was she going to tell the authorities, Sonny?" I ask, leaning over the table.

I stare deep into his eyes and wait for the answer.

15

I leave Sonny with a heavy feeling that he had something to do with Kelly's murder. He said all the right things, looked genuinely surprised and shocked, and still there's this nagging feeling that something isn't right.

When I get back to my desk, I see Thomas standing in the hallway, talking to Captain Medvil.

When the captain storms off, Thomas sees me looking and waves me over. I shake my head no and return my eyes to my laptop, so he approaches me.

"What do you want?" I say without looking up. "I'm very busy."

"Heard you got my case."

"Yeah, I did. Heard you beat up a guy tied to a gurney."

"Yeah. Whatever."

"They have you on tape, you know?" I say. "You can't beat that."

He shrugs again.

"It's all over YouTube, Twitter, and the news."

"Those people, they're just looking for a scapegoat," Thomas quips.

"Yeah. I think attacking some kid who mouthed off to you, that really makes you the victim. Too bad he's in a coma now. Who knows if he'll ever come out."

"Look, I didn't come over here for you to berate me," Thomas says, shifting his weight.

I continue to look at my screen and then slowly raise my eyes up to him.

"This Kelly woman, the one they found in the LA river," Thomas says. "She was married to one of the main guys in the Nighthawks."

"What is that supposed to mean?" I ask.

"All I'm saying is that I would be shocked if this wouldn't have something to do with the club. Beyond shocked, I wouldn't believe it."

"Well, it's a good thing I'm investigating it then, huh?" I say.

He shakes his head.

"If you think that this has something to do with her personal life or someone else and it's not club business, then you're an idiot."

I look up at him, "Look, I'm going to go where the evidence takes me. I'm not going to make assumptions. That's not what good police work is about."

"I'm just warning you. If you start investigating those guys, there's going to be a problem. You're going to need witness protection. No one's going to talk because they'll end up just like Kelly."

Thomas walks away from me just as I'm about to say something else. I hate to admit it, but Thomas is right.

Even though he put on a nice show, it's likely that it was Sonny. It's likely that somebody from that club had something to do with this, especially given how she was dropped off and found in such an experienced kind of manner.

I fill out reports all morning and do all of the grunt work that they never show law enforcement people doing on television. In the afternoon, just as I get that familiar slump where I need a cup of coffee and some sugar to really keep me going, I get a call from Benjamin, the crime tech who asks me to come over.

I head over to his office and find him watching funny videos on YouTube. He doesn't hear me approach and so I watch along with him as an elderly woman tries to pick up her granddaughter, but instead wobbles all around the lawn and falls on an unassuming Labrador retriever. He laughs, and I laugh along with him.

After joking around for a bit, Benjamin gets serious.

“Okay, I have something to tell you.”

“Uh-huh.” I nod, looking down at my phone.

Sydney is calling but I let it go to voice mail.

“So, I found out we got some footage on your victim."

"You did?"

He pulls it up on the screen. "This was taken at a pizza place about ten miles up from where she was found."

"How did you get that?"

"The owner saw her on the news and said that he remembered she was really nice and she left a big tip. She was there alone and here, you see her walking back and forth." He points to the video footage.

The old Chevy Impala keeps driving back and forth across the screen. First, it goes past her, then turns around and goes past her again.

"Do we have her going inside?" I ask.

"Nope." Benjamin shakes his head. "But the date and time match up. Just a few hours before her body was found. I got you the license plate number and searched for the name of the owner."

I smile. He is always two steps ahead.

"Thank you so much, you're the best."

Just as I put out an all-points bulletin, on the vehicle belonging to Jesus

Gutierrez, I get another string of texts.

Where are you?

Call me.

911

Sydney has never sent anything like that before. "Listen, I've got to take this. I'll just be a moment."

"No worries. I got all day," he says casually and flips the screen back to YouTube, digging into his sandwich.

I call Sydney. "What's going on?"

"I'm going into labor. I mean, I'm in labor," she moans into the phone.

"Are you okay?"

"No, I'm at the hospital. Can you come? I can't find Patrick anywhere." I'm about to tell her that I can't come, but then realize that that would put all my priorities out of whack.

My best friend's in labor having her baby three months early. I need to be there. "Cedars-Sinai maternity ward. Just give them my name. I don't know what room I'm in. Hurry."

Her voice sounds faint. Somebody comes into the room and starts to talk in the background. It sounds like the voices of hectic doctors and nurses, and then the phone goes dead.

Without wasting a moment, I drive over there. When I get to the right wing, I run upstairs to the maternity ward and ask the nurse for help in finding her room.

She stops me at first, takes my ID and tells me to calm down. I tell her that my friend is here.

“She's gone into labor way too early.”

The nurse, a woman with a pompous attitude and no chill whatsoever, takes her time checking my identification and everything else. Clearly, she has no sense of urgency. Finally, she tells me to go to the fifth floor, room number 512.

"There's going to be a waiting room out there. You probably shouldn't go into the room quite yet."

I head upstairs and at the nurses' station ask for more details. They go around in circles about how she's my friend and therefore I have no legal right to be told anything about her medical condition. I’m ready for them to pull out a law book to show me what's going on when I see Patrick at the far end of the room.

I run up to him, and he gives me a warm hug. He looks devastated, lost. His eyes don't focus on mine, and he instead looks out somewhere in the distance.

"It's too early. It's too early," he says over and over. He collapses into my arms and I hold him as he sobs.

"I'm really sorry," I whisper.

I hold him for a good five minutes before he gets a hold of himself, and before I get a chance to ask him what's really going on.

"She went into labor. She just had the baby," Patrick says. "They took it. They took her into neonatal intensive care. They haven't said anything else, but the doctor, he didn't look good. He just walked past me as if he didn't want to tell me any news."

"No, maybe you don't know him. Maybe that's not what it means."

"I know exactly what it means, Kaitlyn. I've had that same expression on my face enough times to know what it's like to walk past loved ones of victims and *not* want to talk to them."

The tears dry, and we sit next to each other in the waiting room, just waiting. The sleeve of his shirt is touching mine just a little bit. When I pat the top of this hand, he pulls away slightly but not enough for us not to touch any longer. It's like we need that human contact to make us both feel like maybe it will be okay.

Maybe just this once the worst won't happen.

The day's a blur, and I don't have time to go back to Benjamin to talk to him in person. Instead, we talk on the phone and he gives me the details.

I finally get to see Sydney again that evening. I find her sitting in one of those hospital beds with a fluorescent light above her head. The light hits her face from the top, giving her big circles under her eyes and making her skin appear green and sickly.

"Thank you for coming," she says in a deadpan kind of way, her voice distant and far away.

Patrick sits down next to her.

"Do you know anything about the baby?" I ask.

“She’s okay for now, I guess.” Sydney nods. "I haven't seen her yet, but no one has come to tell me otherwise."

She breaks down crying. Her face scrunches up, and she stops with big fat tears running down her cheeks.

"How did this happen?" I ask.

She shrugs. "I have no idea. I guess she just didn't want to be there anymore."

"No, don't say that," Patrick says lovingly, putting his arm next to his fiancée’s and intertwining their fingers. This is the first time that I've seen him be this loving and present.

"How are you?" I ask when Sydney gets a hold of herself a little bit and wipes some of her tears with the back of her sleeve.

"I'm fine," she mumbles. "Just happened all of a sudden. My water broke and I had the worst pain. Got in the car and decided to drive to the hospital. I thought I was maybe having a miscarriage or something."

She begins to cry again, and it makes me tear up. I get on the other side of her bed, her back is propped up, and I hold her other hand trying to make all of this better.

"I'm so sorry about everything," Sydney says through the tears over and over again. "It's just all my fault. Maybe if I didn't worry so much and work out, maybe if I threw up once in a while and actually had a more painful pregnancy then none of this would have happened."

"That's not how it works," I say, even though I have no idea. Being here with her for forty-five minutes and going through all of these emotions puts my head into a tailspin.

It's not the best feature, but I often can't be around people who are overly emotional because I become consumed by their pain. To deal with it, I just try to stay away, but that doesn't always work. Just as another wave of emotion takes her over, there's a knock at the door, and I manage to say, "Come in."

Dr. Pajir introduces himself and then lays out the details of what happened.

"The baby is doing well, considering the circumstances," he says. "Though she is experiencing some breathing and heart problems."

"How is that doing well?" Patrick glares at him.

"We are not sure what caused the premature delivery since Sydney has not had any of the typical risk factors like smoking, drugs, or IVF, but we will continue to look into it," Dr. Pajir says. "Premature babies may have trouble breathing due to an immature respiratory system. If the baby's lungs lack surfactant — a substance that allows the lungs to expand — she may develop respiratory distress syndrome because the lungs can't expand and contract normally. Premature babies may also develop a lung disorder known as bronchopulmonary dysplasia."

Patrick and I both stare at Dr. Pajir as if he were speaking another language.

"We are currently looking into all of these possibilities," he continues. "And you and your wife are welcome to visit your child if you want to."

16

They don't let me go all the way in to see the baby, but through the little window in the door I see her lying there intubated with wires and tubes, surrounded by a round plastic dome. She looks so small and helpless. When they wheel Sydney in and Patrick wraps his arms around her, I don't think I've ever felt more sorry for a pair of parents.

A nurse comes by and I ask how most of the kids fair and how many of them survive? She looks at me, and she says, "I can't really be certain."

I shuffle away, wanting to avoid the conversation. My phone goes off, and when Sydney looks over at me, dressed in a hospital gown with hair covered and everything else holding on to her little baby's fingers through the plastic enclosure, I give her a little wave and a reassuring nod and she forces a smile. At least she knows that I'm here for her now, despite everything that happened.

I don't take the call in time and it goes straight to voice mail. It's from the office, and they have Jesus in custody.

"Wow, that was quick," I say to myself and shoot Sydney and Patrick a quick text that I have to go to work, but I'll try to be back later.

When I get to the office, I find Jesus sitting in the investigation room cradling a Pepsi.

"Thanks for coming so quickly," Captain Medvil says. "We don't have much to go on, but he's here and he is somewhat willing to talk."

"He is?" I ask.

"Yeah. Looks like it."

Hmm. It was odd. I come in and introduce myself. I shake his hand. He doesn't have an accent and I'm pretty sure that he was born here.

I ask him a little bit about himself and find out that he works on the docks in Long Beach, but has a girlfriend who lives just a mile away from that pizza place where he was spotted.

“So, that's what you were doing there, visiting your girlfriend?"

"I just saw her earlier. She went to work. I hung around, got some pizza. That's it," Jesus says.

"Do you happen to know anything about this woman?" I take out a picture of Kelly Flynn from my folder.

"No, just saw her on the news."

"So is that a no, or you saw her on the news?" I press.

"Well, you know how it is," he says, finishing the can and then crushing it against the table. I haven't seen anyone do that in years.

"I've seen her on the news," he admits. "What does this have to do with me?"

"Well, we saw your car driving back and forth in front of the pizza place. Kind of suspicious."

"What? I can't make a mistake? Go one way and then another?" He looks at me, narrowing his eyes.

It's hard to know which direction to go with when you first meet a person. You can come on strong like you know everything.

You can come on like you don't know much. Maybe they'll share something. In this case, I feel like I played the wrong hand.

“So, you are the owner of the 2006 Chevy Impala?” I try another angle.

"Yes. So what?"

"And this is your car driving past the pizza place, right?"

“Yes again.”

"I just find it curious because she walked right out here, right up front. You see?"

I rewind a little bit and show him.

His face drops.

"And then just a moment later, you turned your car around and you drove all the way back. What was so urgent that you drove past her, you saw her, and then what? You just decided to maybe have some fun with her?"

"No, I have a girlfriend."

"No, he doesn't," Captain Medvil says into my ear.

I'm taken a bit aback by his gruff voice, and he even clears his throat as he talks, making me recoil more. I adjust my hair, making sure that it's covering my earpiece, and take a sip of my Starbucks coffee to show him that I'm just distracted by my drink.

"As it turns out, you don't have a girlfriend, right?" I say.

He stares at me, blinking a few times.

"He used to have a girlfriend, but they broke up three months ago," Captain Medvil says into my ear. They had a deputy interview her just a little bit ago to confirm the story.

I relay this to Jesus, who blinks at me again and then crosses his arms across his chest.

"What were you doing there, Jesus? You can tell me."

"Really? I can tell *you*?" he says, throwing his chin up in the air. "Please."

He's dressed in a nice pair of jeans and a hoodie. Clean, modest, but nothing flamboyant or particularly fashionable. His information sheet says that he's forty-five but he could pass for his early thirties with that attractive smile and mischievous grin.

"Look." I change my tactic. I was being a little forward earlier and I pull it back. I want him to think I'm his friend. "You can tell me anything that happened, okay? I'm on your side."

"You're on my side? Please. You're a cop."

I nod.

"I know, but if something happened that was an accident, or you just saw her, she got into your car willingly, you were flirting. Whatever might've happened, I want you to tell me the truth. I'm not going to automatically think that you did something bad, but I do right now. That's why I need an explanation."

His demeanor changes a little bit. He adjusts his position in the chair. I continue to talk. I try to give him ways out.

"Listen, you're an attractive guy. You know that, right?" He smiles at me and winks. "Of course you do. Someone a girl would be lucky to have a date with."

"Are you flirting with me, Detective Carr?" He leans over the table, looking a little bit too eager.

"No, not at all. But I'm talking to you as a friend."

That word couldn't be more disingenuous and untrue, but somehow when I deliver the line, it feels like it could be. That's why I end up doing a lot of interrogations in the department.

People open up to me. Some of my colleagues joke around that I should have been a psychologist instead of a detective, but then again, maybe having someone like me instead of someone who will break some skulls is a good look for the LAPD.

"So did you happen to see her? Did she get in your car?" I ask.

"I don't know what you're talking about," he says after a long pause, just as I feel like he's about to come clean.

"Well, you can play it like that, Jesus, but the thing is that we have your car. We're taking it in for DNA and fingerprints as we speak."

The blood drains away from his face. When he looks up at me, his eyes don't focus. His irises keep bouncing from side to side, like little ping-pong balls.

"So, is there anything that you want to tell me before we find out what we have there?"

"Look, she got in my car, okay?" he says.

I stiffen my grip on the coffee cup and carefully place it back down. I don't want him to know that I'm getting any new information that I don't already have.

"She was walking by. I saw her in the pizza shop. We talked a little bit, kind of flirted, so then when I drove past her and rolled down the window and said, 'Do you want a ride somewhere?' she got in."

"Just like that?" I ask.

"Yeah. Just like that."

"Okay. Go on."

"That's why you're going to find her fingerprints inside my car, but that's it. Nothing happened. I gave her a ride."

"Where did you give her a ride to?"

He hesitates. He clearly can't say her apartment because I don't think he knows where she lives. "Just the park. The one a couple of blocks away."

"That's where she was going?" I ask.

"Yeah," he says, not at all convincingly.

"Listen, Jesus. You have to tell me the truth. This girl, she was found murdered and rolled up in a tarp in the bottom of the LA River."

"What?" he asks, but he doesn't seem at all surprised. "I had nothing to do with that."

"Are you sure? I mean, we have her DNA evidence in your car and you just admitted to giving her a ride."

"No, nothing happened."

"So you dropped her off at the park?" I ask.

"Yeah."

"So, when we search your car, we're *not* going to find any blood?"

His eyes continue to ping-pong from side to side, and he swallows hard. "She had a cut on her finger," he says after a very long pause. "If you find any blood, it might be from that."

"Okay, good job. Now keep him talking," Captain Medvil says into my ear.

That's how you do it, classic interrogation technique, something I learned a long time ago and am surprised it keeps working.

You stay one step ahead of the suspect. If you want him to say that someone was with him in the car, you say that you already have the DNA evidence there. Then he has to explain it away.

Once I have Kelly in the car with him, then I mention that she might be bleeding. If he were giving her a ride, why would she be bleeding? So he tries to explain it away with a finger cut.

The only problem with this whole confession is, of course, the fact that I have absolutely no DNA evidence. Not yet. I didn't even have enough for a warrant to search his car.

The only reason why Jesus is in here in the first place is because he came in voluntarily for a chat. Well, one thing is for sure. I'm definitely going to be able to get that warrant to search his car now, check it for fibers, fingerprints, and of course fluids.

“Now, how about this, Jesus? Do you have any reason as to why your DNA would be found on or inside Kelly Flynn’s body?"

"No."

"Are you sure?" I ask. "Because you know consensual sex is not illegal, but raping someone is, and killing someone certainly is."

"Okay, fine. Fine," he says. "We had sex, okay? She was really friendly, flirtatious. We had a good time. We just pulled over and did it by the park."

I stare at him.

"Okay. Why don't you stay here, I'm going to get some paperwork to fill out and I'll be back with you in a bit?”

17

I walk out of the interrogation room feeling as high as a kite. I can't believe that this just happened. Did he really just say everything that I think he said? A couple of doors down is the room where everyone gathers to watch the live feed.

As soon as I walk in, everyone congratulates me and breaks into a big round of applause.

“You did a good job there, Kaitlyn,” Captain Medvil says.

“I can't believe that I got him to say all that stuff,” I admit.

"Listen, if anyone can do it, you can. You've got the magic touch."

He winks at me and the other detectives in the room give me a little scowl.

"Well, I got him to admit to all of that stuff, but now we'll have to check the car to see if any of it's true," I say because, of course, we hadn't run any of the tests yet. All that I told Jesus was nothing but a lie.

"You need to go back out there and keep on talking," Captain Medvil says. "Find out more about him. Get him comfortable. He admitted to having sex with her. Now you need to get him to confess to the rest."

I use the restroom and look at myself in the mirror afterward as I wash my hands. I have dark circles under my eyes and my hair is limp and lifeless. The harsh fluorescent lighting doesn't help matters, of course.

Something about that conversation doesn't feel right to me.

I mean, I'm as happy as anyone else about the confession, if it's true, but what if it's not?

I dry my hands, use the paper towel to open the door, and then toss it in the trash behind me.

When I walk back into the interrogation room with Jesus, I plaster a concerned, but not an overly eager expression on my face.

“How are you doing, Jesus? Can I get you something to eat, drink?”

"Sure, my stomach is rumbling," he says.

I walk out to the vending machine and get him the chips and pretzels that he requested, grabbing a bag for myself as well.

Nobody likes to eat alone. Right?

"So tell me about yourself, Jesus," I say, popping open my bag. He breaks into his and quickly devours at least half of it before answering.

"Been living in Long Beach all my life. Came here when I was little with my parents from south Mexico."

“Okay, do you mind if I ask if you have a driver's license and if you're in the country legally?”

He hesitates. “Why does it always have to come down to *that*?”

“The only reason I'm asking is that I want to tell you that you have nothing to worry about. I don't care about the border patrol. I am a detective. I'm looking to solve this murder, so I'm not going to report you to anyone if that's what you're worried about.”

He sits back in his chair, feeling a little bit more comfortable. Usually people use the immigration status to threaten suspects into making confessions.

We talk about growing up in Los Angeles and what it was like and he relaxes even more. Then I take the conversation back to Kelly.

"Can you tell me more about what happened between you two?" I ask. This time, however, he refuses to say a word.

"I already said too much. I've seen Dateline. I shouldn't have even said any of it."

“Jesus," I interrupt him.

He looks startled.

"I'm here for you. I just want to find out what happened to Kelly. I don't want to jam you up if you had nothing to do with it, but I need your help. You said that you had sex with her in the car, by the park, right? What happened after?"

"I don't know," he says with a shrug.

"I think you do. We found her body in the LA River."

"You think I *killed* her?" he asks. "Is this what this is really about?"

"I don't know. So far. You're the last person to have seen her alive."

"Okay. Fine. Let's say that I did."

"Was it an accident?" I ask.

I always like to give people I talk to an out. That keeps them going. They say more, digging themselves into a bigger hole.

"Did something happen by any chance? Did she get hurt, and you didn't mean for it to happen?"

"Yeah, she liked it rough," he says without blinking. "She wanted me to hold her down, force myself onto her. She had this rape fantasy, whatever the hell that is."

I tilt my head. "What happened exactly?"

"I put my hands around her throat. I pushed her down, and I started to strangle her. She really liked it. She told me to keep going. So we started having sex."

I look at him and the kind, open to listening expression on my face changes as all blood drains away. "Do you think I'm an idiot, Jesus?"

"What?" He shrugs.

"You're telling me that you strangled her?"

"Yeah."

"Kelly Flynn was shot in the head execution-style, back of the head, right by the neck. She was not strangled. I've got the medical examiner's report to prove it."

He tilts his head to one side and smiles.

"What are you doing?" I ask.

"Just taking you for a little ride."

I shake my head and I start to see little dots in the corners of my eyes. Is this really happening?

"You're wasting my time."

"Look, I don't know what you want me to say." He laughs.

"I want you to tell me the truth."

"Well, the truth is that I never saw her. You can't possibly have her DNA in my car because she never got in it. She never cut her finger. We never flirted. I never even met her. The first time I've seen her is when you showed me her picture.

"But that's how you play this game, isn't it, Detective? You pick up some brown guy off the street who was driving in the area for no reason. Someone points him out to you and you narrow your search onto him. He must have done it. Why not? It's the only lead you have, but wait, wasn't she also divorced? How about the ex-husband? Why not him? Why try to pin a case on someone like that when you can go after a soft target like me, lie to me about what you have, scare me, ask me casually about my immigration status like you actually care. Well, guess what? I am legal in this country. I am a citizen, and I'm a veteran, too. I served in the Iraq War and in Afghanistan. So you can just go fuck yourself."

He stands up to leave. I do as well.

"Am I under arrest, Detective?" he asks.

"No."

"Good, then I'm out of here."

He heads toward the door. I have nothing to hold him on but we still have the car.

"Tell him to stop," Captain Medvil says over and over in my ear, but I just turn off the earpiece and let him walk out.

Afterward, the captain pulls me into his office to vent.

"Look, you were there. You saw every interrogation tactic that I used. They all worked, but he was onto us. He was just having a little fun."

"You should have stopped him from walking away. You shouldn't have let him make such fools out of us."

"What was I supposed to do? Arrest him? On what charge exactly? We have no DNA evidence from his car. We have to get those fingerprints. We have to get those fluids. And you and I both know that that's highly unlikely."

Two days later, the results are confirmed. Jesus Gutierrez had nothing to do with anything. His car was at the scene, but a vintage clothing store from across the street submitted their recordings, and you clearly see him just driving up one direction, turning around and driving past Kelly on the way back.

Jesus was right. We had nothing because he didn't do anything. The thought that he could have confessed to a crime he didn't commit, and that something like that happens all the time, many times over, all over the United States, sent a chill through my body. This guy was smart, but many aren't. Many fall for cops telling them lies and say things that they shouldn't, even placing themselves at scenes where they never were.

I never want to be someone who elicits a false confession. I want the truth, but the problem is that as someone in my position, you have to pull and jerk on certain strings, hoping that one of them unravels and leads you to the truth. That's not always the case.

My thoughts return to the two men in Kelly's life, Sonny, her ex-husband, and Logan, the man that she'd met at the beach with whom she had that connection. I need to talk to both of them again, but so far there's nothing to go on. She wasn't killed at the location where she was found and that makes the search particularly difficult.

18

I have the next few days off and I spend them at home relaxing but my mind remains at work. I keep thinking about Sonny and Logan and how one of them is a potential killer and how little I have to go on. More videotapes come in and are being processed by Benjamin and the rest of the crime technicians. But this is a case of having too much information to go through.

There are lots of tips being called in. Kelly was a pretty, young blonde woman after all, and those tend to catch people's attention. The tips all have to be replied to and investigated and pursued further to see if any of them are possibilities. But I'm off right now and after working so many days in a row, I decide that I need to actually take care of myself. I keep in touch with Captain Talarico up in Big Bear, but the toxicology report isn't back yet on Natalie. They're backed up at the lab, going through a round of layoffs and they have a lot of cases to go through.

On my days off, I go to the hospital and visit Sydney who is looking better and better every day. They named the baby Sophie, and even though she's still in that little plastic incubator cooking like an egg, she is looking better. Patrick is there all the time.

He's bringing food and things and just hanging out with Sydney. I've actually never seen him that caring before. I know that she told me that there was a side to him that I hadn't seen, that he was actually very sweet and kind, and not the lying and cheating dog that he seemed to be.

I see the way that he looks at Sophie and at Sydney and how caring and protective he is with both of them. Despite the fact that I don't want to like him, I find myself giving him a chance.

The hospital's cold, and I always wear an extra sweater when I go there. Sydney sits dressed in layers, too. Today she's officially getting released and will then have to come back and visit Sophie on her own.

"How's everything with work?" she asks.

I shrug and give her an update on what has happened with the Kelly Flynn case.

"Wow, that really sucks."

"Just hate wasting my time with that interrogation. I'm glad it didn't lead to any false confession, but that guy was playing with fire. Some other cop would have definitely put him behind bars for something."

"So you released him? He had nothing to do with it?"

"Nope. They kept the car, ran the prints. Got a warrant because he did confess initially. So that was enough, luckily, but he was right. We didn't find anything in his car. And there's that other angle from another camera where she just walked past it, never got in or even approached."

"So, you really don't think that he had anything to do with this?" Sydney asks.

"No, I don't. I mean, it would be very unlikely, but they definitely didn't meet then."

"What's your gut telling you?" Sydney asks.

"I have to go back to the drawing board."

We talk in circles for a while and then I ask her about her work.

"Well, I have maternity leave a little bit for this time and, you know, however long it takes. Sophie has to reach some milestones before they let her leave."

“So, she doesn’t have to be here the full two months until her due date?” I ask.

“No, not at all. But she has to be able to be in the car seat and to be able to maintain her body temperature in an open crib before she can go home. And afterward, she might have some issues. I've been reading about preemies and they have a lot of trouble sleeping. They're usually delayed developmentally, but that doesn't mean that they can't catch up.”

I nod, reaching over and taking her hand into mine and giving her a light squeeze. "It's going to be okay, and I'm going to be here for you."

"Really? You're going to be here overnight? You want to sleep over and take care of a screaming baby?"

I laugh. "Well, maybe not *there* for you, but during the days you can definitely count on me."

She smiles. "Your days off, you mean?"

I tilt my head to one side and give her a wink.

She knows exactly how unreliable and busy our work schedules can be, how many hours we have to put in, and how much overtime is expected. It doesn't exactly make for a lot of family time.

I'm glad that she's thinking ahead, planning for crying and possible problems with eating and all the other issues that Sophie might have, rather than the alternative: her not being here at all.

I read something about premature babies as well, and sometimes they don't make it, but I don't dare to bring that up.

THE NEXT WEEK goes by uneventfully. I'm busy with other cases and Luke gets back, but is busy with work as well. We see each other when our schedules line up and it still feels weird that we are living together. I visit Sydney, Patrick, and Sophie, and for a while there it's a regular work week.

When Sydney and I grab some coffee together after one of my visits, she surprises me. I order a latte and she gets a cappuccino as well as a cake pop.

"You want one?" she asks.

"No, thanks." I shake my head.

"I have some news." She smiles.

"Oh, yeah?"

"Yeah. We decided to scrap the whole wedding."

"You did?" I ask.

"It's just too much given what happened with Sophie and it's like, who cares about a party inviting all these family members that I don't really like, paying for all of them to eat and party and then judge me? I was so set on how important that is to, you know, solidify our relationship or something, and now I just know that I want to be with Patrick and we want to be husband and wife and the best parents that we can be to little Sophie."

"That's great," I say after I take a moment to take in the news.

"I mean, all of these medical bills are going to be a lot. I don't even know how are we going to pay for all of this. I mean, Cedars-Sinai and the NICU unit, but it's worth it if they save her life."

"Of course it is."

"It's not just finances though. It's like, I just don't want to deal with the event planning, you know? Like, who cares about dressing up and being pretty and putting on this whole show?"

"No, I totally understand," I say, as someone who's not a big fan of lavish weddings and huge displays of affection. "I totally get it. Well, I'm really happy for you."

Just in that moment, Patrick appears in the doorway. She waves to him through the busy Starbucks. He comes over and gives her a kiss and flashes me a smile.

"Did you tell her?" he asks.

Sydney nods and leans against his shoulder.

"Well, what do you think?" she asks.

"Um, I think this is great news. I mean, congratulations."

"So, will you do it?" he asks.

"Oh, I didn't get to that part yet." She smiles and laughs that high-pitched, giggly, kind of school girl laugh that I haven't heard from Sydney in a long time.

"What are you talking about?" I turn to her.

She pushes her thick, dark hair out of her face, leans over, and asks, "Will you be my maid-of-honor?"

"Yes, of course. I mean, I already said I would."

"Today. We're going to the courthouse. Will you be a witness?"

"Right now? You're going to get married right now?" I ask, repeating myself.

"Yeah."

"Um, yeah, sure."

"It's not too far from here. You said that you had some time, right?"

"Yeah, I do."

"So I thought that instead of going to the bookstore and just hanging out, you would do this with us instead."

"Luke is going to be there, too," Patrick interjects. "He's meeting us. He's going to be my best man."

I look at them, happy as can be, and I smile a big, wide smile. My whole face lights up. I'm genuinely happy for them. This feels like a fresh new start. I hope that they are happy for a lifetime.

I follow them in my car, keenly aware of the fact that I'm not exactly dressed for anything, well, besides court. I'm wearing a black suit, matching pants and a stiff, white-collared blouse. When we get to the courthouse where we've all been a million times, testifying at various trials, it suddenly feels like a different place altogether.

"Judge Maloney is going to be doing it." Sydney smiles.

He's one of the most fair and even-tempered judges in town and everyone likes him. Even the criminal defense attorneys.

I follow Sydney into the bathroom where she changes into a simple, white dress, cut at her knees with just a little bit of ruching around her collar bone. She puts a flower behind her ear and re-applies a little bit of lipstick.

"You look stunning," I say. "First of all, I can't believe that you just had a baby a week ago. You look absolutely beautiful."

She laughs and gives me a brief hug. "Thank you for being here. I don't think I could do this without you, any of it."

"You're the best friend that any girl could have," I whisper in her ear, squeezing her hand again.

"Do you think I'm making the right decision?" she asks as we walk over the threshold holding hands.

It's not one of those questions where she sounds like she's hesitating. She wants to hear only one answer and luckily, I have the right one.

"Yes. This last week, I saw how much he loves you and Sophie and how caring he's been. It seems like he has really changed. He's become a different person from who he was before."

"I feel like that, too." She smiles.

We run into Luke outside the judge's chambers, and he takes me into his arms and gives me a soft, warm kiss that makes me light up from the inside out. He's dressed in the suit that he was wearing earlier in the day, professional but, nevertheless, extremely attractive. His hair is a little bit tossed and his eyes twinkle under the fluorescent lights.

"I've missed you," he whispers when Judge Maloney opens the door and welcomes us inside.

The only person he doesn't know is Luke and they exchange quick handshakes and brief hellos.

"I've missed you, too," I mouth to him as we watch our friends get married.

He adds, "I want this," and I whisper back, "Me, too."

19

Over the next week, I try to talk to Logan but every time I check in on him at his apartment he's not there. I follow up with Sonny as well without much luck. The one time I do meet with him right outside his house, he suddenly cuts me off and says that I need to go through his lawyer.

"I just can't keep answering questions like this," he says. "If you have anything specific, call him."

This isn't exactly the ideal situation and the Kelly Flynn case is going cold. The DNA and fingerprint evidence came back from the car. Kelly was never in Jesus's car.

I meet up with Catherine Harris, the assistant DA, after we run into each other at the Starbucks down the street. I haven't seen her in a while after our rather intense previous conversation where we both shared a lot about our one commonality, which was Thomas Abrams.

"How are you doing?" she asks.

I update her about what's happening with my sister's case as well as Kelly Flynn.

"What's your gut telling you?" she asks.

"That I have no idea who could have done it or why. It's definitely an execution-style killing and the ex-husband has a motive. He wanted full custody of their kid, which he now has."

"What about the new boyfriend?" she asks.

"I don't know, but then again, I don't really know him. He was in foster care. He doesn't have many connections. I don't know much about their relationship except for what he told me. But he does seem like kind of an unlikely person to murder her like that in cold blood."

"So you're thinking the ex-husband?"

"I am but I have no evidence. We were following the lead about this guy who was seen in the vicinity," I say and tell her about Jesus. "But it wasn't him."

I ask her about her work and she says that she has a lot of cases.

"What about the private firm?" I ask, something that she had mentioned earlier.

"Definitely still an option." She nods. "I'm thinking about it. The workload is a lot less but I'd definitely be paid a lot better and they like to hire district attorneys because you have inside information about how the city operates."

"What do you mean?" I ask.

"Well, not so much inside information but connections to people who still work at the department. I know the judges. I know how they think and how they might rule. That kind of thing."

Our conversation drifts from work to other topics. She knows about Sydney so I tell her about the premature birth and she says that she's going to send flowers and stop by.

We're becoming closer now, more like friends rather than colleagues. I enjoy talking to her because she's someone who understands what it's like to work in this field, a very male-dominated place. Besides that, she also knows the truth about Thomas.

"I've come to a decision," Catherine says, tapping her manicured fingers on the Formica tabletop.

Our eyes meet and I like the winged eyeliner and the generally perfect way in which all of her makeup is applied. There are highlights on the bridge of her nose, lowlights elsewhere, but yet it's not so much that it looks like she's overly made up.

"What kind of decision?" I ask.

"About Thomas," she says after a beat.

She presses her lips together, puckering them in almost a nervous fashion. "I'm going to talk to Internal Affairs about my experience with him."

Suddenly my head begins to buzz.

I've been thinking about this as well but I haven't had the courage to actually come right out and decide to do it.

“He's being investigated for beating up that suspect who was handcuffed to the gurney; that video's everywhere,” I say. “The department can't cover it up. He's going to have certain consequences for what he did.”

"Yeah, I saw that. I'm glad that they caught that on tape. Our higher ups aren't exactly happy about it," Catherine says, "but I am. It shows his temper and how volatile and out of control he can get over well, basically nothing. Internal Affairs is launching an investigation. I know that I haven't come forward about his abuse but I think it's time for me to make a statement. I just want it on the record, what he did and how violent he was because all of these little breadcrumbs, they lead to certain decisions being made. And I have to tell you, I couldn't live with it if he had gone out there and shot some kid or anyone over a $20 bill or something stupid like that. He could easily be that cop on the news and I can't have that on my conscience. I can't cover up what he did to me. I want this on record. I'll testify. I'll tell them what happened and they can make the decision."

"I think that's really brave," I say, after a long pause.

I grasp onto my grande green iced tea and feel the condensation and the water droplets underneath my fingertips.

"I'm not asking you to do the same thing," Catherine says. "I know that you're in a different position than I am because, well, you're technically colleagues in the same department."

"Yeah, but I know where you're coming from. This stuff has to be in his file so that people don't think that he just lost it in that one moment. The public has to know that this is a pattern of behavior. That kid's in a coma because of a few curse words? How is that fair? Cops like Thomas need to have better control of their emotions and not fly off the handle over nothing. In this job, you are confronted with a lot of chances to lose it and you just can't go there."

"How do you deal with it?" Catherine asks.

"It's a mindset," I say with a shrug. "You can't let other people bring you down. No matter what name someone calls you, no matter how pissed off they make you, you can't just punch them. You can't shoot them. Those are just words they're throwing at you and you can't have that kind of reaction."

"I don't think he's cut out for this job," Catherine says. "He's not someone who can just let things slide off. He doesn't have thick skin. Everything pisses him off."

"So, you're going to tell Internal Affairs *everything*?" I ask.

"I've covered up for him enough and they're making this decision about what to do with him. I'm not trying to get him fired. I just feel like they need to have all the facts."

"I guess I need to think about this," I say.

"Of course, I'd be lying if I didn't tell you that I'd love for you to talk to them as well. Then at least there'd be two of us. Corroboration and that kind of thing but I understand if you can't."

"Yeah, I mean we work together and no one knows that we have a past. It's very complicated."

"I know it is," she says, reaching over and squeezing my hand.

Touching her makes me feel incredibly guilty. There is a lot to talk about, think about.

"I'd be lying if I didn't say that I want him off the force," I confess.

I finish the last of my drink and pick at the muffin that we got to share. It's moist and the blueberries look awfully fresh but suddenly I've lost my appetite.

"It's just that people don't know that we were even dating. People look at you differently when they know about your personal life. I'm friendly with some and I guess it would be fine if they knew but there's just this professional relationship I have with all the others and I'm worried about how it's going to affect my career."

"Yeah, I know." She nods.

"I mean, I don't have any offers from any fancy firms. This is it for me and if I go ahead and come clean about this thing that happened, people are going to look at me differently. I know that Internal Affairs says that everything we tell them is confidential but people talk. There are lots of leaks in this ship, unfortunately."

"Okay, I get it."

Catherine tosses her hair from one side to the other.

"Listen, I'm going to give him my statement this week. You do what you think is right. I'm with you either way."

"Thanks." I nod. "I appreciate that."

I'm thankful for the fact that she doesn't push me further but what she doesn't say, and something that we both know, is that Thomas is going to be put on trial for punching that kid on the gurney, the kid's family is pushing for it and so is the public.

The department doesn't really want to pursue it but public opinion is making it difficult to drop it. There could be a plea deal that would be somewhat favorable to him and a plea deal is always based on prior history, prior evidence of who Thomas is as a person. My statement to Internal Affairs would go a long way to making a plea deal that would actually involve pushing him off the force.

20

The next time I have two days off, I head up to Big Bear. I don't tell Mom in advance and immediately regret it.

I use my own key to get in, just as her friend comes out wearing her bathrobe pinched tight around his substantial body. We both jump back and I rush out of the house, shaking my head and repeating the word “No," over and over again.

"What are you doing here?" Mom emerges a few minutes later.

"Who is that?" I ask.

"It's none of your business. He's a friend of mine."

"Yeah, you're right. Sorry, I should've called."

"Of course you should've called. I didn't even know you were coming to visit."

"I just had some time off and haven't been up here for a bit, so I thought I'd stop by."

"Well, not every time is good for me, you know. I have a life."

"Yeah, I can see that." I nod again.

I stand on the porch a little bit, but flurries begin to fall. I cross my arms and hold myself tightly.

"Do you want me to leave?" I ask, shifting my weight from one foot to the other, keenly aware of the fact that I again need to change out of my ballet flats into something a little bit more substantial for the mountains.

"Just wait in the living room. We're going to get decent, okay? I've wanted you to meet him, but definitely not this way. I guess life had other plans."

A few minutes later, Mom comes out dressed in an oversized sweater and a casual pair of sweatpants that I've never seen her wear in front of company before.

She then introduces her guy friend as Danny Weidner. When I come back inside and look at him closer, I have a faint memory of meeting him before.

"Were you ever friends with my dad?" I ask.

"Kaitlyn!" Mom yells from the other room.

"No, it's okay, honey." He uses a warm tone with her like this is something that's been going on for a while. "Yeah, we used to be friends. You could say we knew each other well."

"Friends? What kind of friends? Did you sell drugs as well?"

"Kaitlyn, if you're going to be rude, you're going to have to see yourself out!" Mom yells from the kitchen, still working on getting coffee, tea, and cookies ready. "What are you even doing here? I told you that you have to let me know when you want to come over."

"Actually, you said no such thing," I say. "I thought you'd be happy to see your oldest daughter."

I'm tempted to use the phrase only daughter, but I don't want to throw salt on the wound.

"You and I have something in common," Danny says, adjusting his stance in the old recliner in the living room.

He's a broad-shouldered guy with a receding hairline and a big belly that hangs over his belt.

At least he's age appropriate, I say to myself, and not some twenty-five-year-old like I thought maybe she would take up with just to piss me off.

When the coffee, tea, and cookies are ready, we sit down awkwardly at the coffee table and Danny tells me that he has known my parents for a long time.

“We have something in common, Kaitlyn," he says again, shoving a big cookie into his mouth and catching the crumbs underneath his chin.

"Oh, yeah? What's that?"

"Well, we're both in law enforcement, or I was until retirement."

"What do you mean?" I ask, leaning forward, having no appetite for the chocolate chip cookies that Mom pushes toward me.

"Well, I used to work for the sheriff's department. I know Captain Talarico well. We're old chums."

I narrow my eyes. “So, when you say you know my dad?"

"Yeah, more in the professional manner, but we got friendly."

"How is that?" I say.

"Well, he worked with our department. He was a nice guy outside of his illegal activities. Really easy to like."

"What are you trying to say?" I ask, putting my cup down on the saucer. Danny looks over at my mom, who gives him a slight nod.

"He was an informant. He worked with a buddy of mine mainly, but I handled him once in a while. In addition to selling drugs, he also had a big bookie operation, but he was useful in that he told us a lot about the other bookies in the area. And so we learned a lot about how certain illegal activities came to operate."

My mouth gets dry. I sit back against the couch.

"Did you know about this, Mom?" I ask. She nods. "Why didn't you ever tell me about any of it?"

"You know how talking about your father is difficult for me. I thought that you knew enough already, and it gave you a bad feeling about him."

"But it's the truth, Mom. I have to know the truth."

"No, not necessarily. It's difficult to know the truth about those you love. I wanted to protect you."

"I'm an adult, Mom. You can't just hide things."

"I'm not hiding it. And besides, here we are. You're hearing the truth. You like what you're hearing?" she challenges me.

Of course, I don't. I don't like any of it. In fact, I hate it. She knows that as well as I do. It's not nice to hear that your father was a bookie and was an informant for the police.

"What else are you hiding from me?" I ask, sitting on the edge of the ratty couch, the one that has been here my whole life.

"God, nothing changes at all," I say, inching toward the edge of the seat. "You've always kept secrets from me. You've always pretended that our family was something special, something that it wasn't. And when I called you on it, you made it seem like I was making stuff up. That's called gaslighting."

"I was just trying to protect you," she hisses. "You don't want to be rude in front of our guest."

"Our guest? More like *your* guest."

"Look, I know that you're mad at your mother, but you should give her some slack," Danny says, talking to me as if we've been friends for years.

"No." I point my finger in his face, the lavender nail polish on my nail peeling in parts. "She has been keeping secrets from me my whole life. I need to know what happened to my father."

"I don't know about that," Danny says, "but I can tell you that he was one of the biggest bookies in the mountains, if not down in San Bernardino. He took everyone's bets, and the way that he grew his business was by reporting on others. Nobody wants to hear that, but that's the god-awful truth. He was a nice guy, too. Real friendly, easygoing."

“When did he become an informant?" I ask.

"We pinched him. He was facing five to seven years for a robbery he was part of and he offered. We had no idea that he was a bookie. He was real good at it. He worked with a few other people who covered for him. He did all his work in the shadows."

"And you knew this, Mom?” I ask, sitting back a little bit, trying to relax, but knowing that something like this is going to weigh heavily on me for a long time.

"Yeah, I did. And before you get mad, I didn't tell you to protect you. You were already so angry. You were an angry child. You were an angry teenager."

"That's because you were *lying* to me."

"I know. But the angrier you got, the less I wanted to share. I also wanted you to keep some good feelings about your father. Despite all of his flaws and shortcomings, he loved you very much. He cared about you. He worried about you and yeah, he didn't want me to tell you."

"He didn't?"

"Of course not. We were raising you differently. There are some mobsters who are proud of it, who want everyone to know. Your father wasn't like that. He wanted to keep it a secret from you. He knew that it would hurt you deeply to know that he did what he did."

I finish my tea, excuse myself from the table, and walk out onto the porch. I need some fresh air. A few minutes later, Mom follows me out.

"How long have you been seeing him?" I ask.

"For a while. Since before Violet disappeared."

"Really?"

"Yeah. I was friends with his wife and she died of cancer a couple of years ago. We connected in church. We both went to the same support group. You know me, I'm not very religious, but I needed someone to talk to about just feeling depressed and that kind of thing."

The fresh air coming off the mountains gives me a burst of energy. Mom pops in to grab her jacket, and we sit on the swing out front. We used to sit like this a lot when I was little, but I don't remember sitting here once since Violet disappeared.

"Look, I'm sorry that you caught us like that," she says after a long pause.

We push off at the same time, allowing the momentum of the wooden swing to carry us forward. It creaks with each movement, and the predictability of it is peaceful and kind of relaxing.

"You shouldn't have seen me like that with Danny, but I haven't told you about him because of Violet's disappearance. Since then, we just never seemed to be on the right page. It didn't seem appropriate to talk about my love life."

I want to bring up the fact that I've talked about mine plenty, and that would have been a good opening, but I know that she likes to keep things to herself.

"So, Dad was really an informant?" I ask.

"Yes. There's one cop that he worked with in particular. You should talk to him. His name is JD Ryder. He was your dad's friend. He was also the guy he worked with most closely when he worked as an informant."

I nod.

"I don't want you to think too harshly of your father," Mom adds. "He did what he did to spend time with you and me. He did it for his family."

"Look, I don't have a whole thing about cooperating with the police like all those criminals have. It's not like I think he was a snitch or anything."

"I know, but there's still some sort of law and certain rules that people abide by. And I want you to know that your dad wasn't perfect, but he loved you and he loved your sister and he loved me. And we were happy for many years."

"Even when he lost all the money? Even when you had all those fights about him selling drugs?"

"Yes, even then," she says, raising one eyebrow. "I don't talk about that often. You know how difficult it is for me to speak about Hal."

This is the first time that she's used his name, and it takes me by surprise. "But the truth is that we were what we were. We loved each other how we could. I know that you're out there looking for this perfect man, for this perfect love, and maybe your father and I were not perfect, but we were perfect for each other. But if you want to know more about him, you contact JD. He can help."

"Okay. I appreciate that," I say. "What about you and Danny?"

"Danny has been very helpful with everything that's been going on with Violet. He's been talking with the sheriff's department, conducting some of his own investigation."

"And?" I ask.

"Well, nothing. He doesn't have any more answers than anyone else. But he's been here for me and I want you to respect that. Do you understand?"

I nod. I shuffle my feet along the floorboards as the swing goes back and forth. We sit in silence for a while.

I appreciate her and Danny telling me all of this about my father, things that I did not know about until now. I wish I could have found this out sooner, but of course you get the truth when you get it, and you should be thankful to get it at all.

As we sit on the porch and talk a little bit about everything, I ask her about the mortgage. I helped her out with it a little bit ago, but she hasn't asked about more help since.

"Actually, Danny has been helping me pay the bills. He's got a retirement fund and he paid off his house a while ago."

"Does he live here?" I ask.

She shakes her head.

"No, he just stays. He has his old house. We're taking it slowly. Neither of us have lived with anyone else of the opposite sex since our spouses and, I don't know, it just feels weird."

"But he's helping you pay your bills?"

"Yes. He's really good to me, Kaitlyn. I haven't gambled in a while. I deleted all those apps off my phone, no poker, no Texas Hold 'em. I don't play anything anymore because they trigger me."

"Good. I'm really glad about that," I say.

"You'll give him a chance, right?"

"Yeah, I guess," I mumble, not being particularly firm one way or another.

"I want you to give him a chance for real."

"Okay," I say after a quick thought. "Yes, I'm glad that you have someone in your life, Mom. I just wish that you could've told me earlier. I just wish that we were in a better place, you know?"

"Yeah, me, too."

"Well, we can work on that. I promise."

She smiles, reaches over, and squeezes my hand.

21

Mom invites me back inside after we both get chilled, but I make a lame excuse and get back in my car, telling her that I have something to do. I don't. I drive around the lake for a while, two circles at least, doing nothing in particular. I keep thinking about what she told me, what they both said, and all of these secrets that my family has held onto for far too long.

I stop by a gas station to fill up the tank and then search the name that she'd given me on my phone: JD Ryder, retired sheriff's investigator. It doesn't take me long to find him or his address.

My second loop around the lake, I decide to pop into the sheriff's office and find Captain Talarico grabbing a snack by the vending machine. I've seen him here enough to know that the pretzels are his go-to, even though the Lay's potato chips are his favorite.

We catch up, talk about the weather, nothing in particular, dancing around the topic of Natalie's dead body and my sister's disappearance. He'd called me and given me the news, or pretty much lack thereof.

"It's good to see you, but no updates so far."

"Are you going to bring Neil in again?"

"No," he says, shaking his head and popping open the bag of pretzels. "His father is corralling the troops," he says. "Unless we have something serious, he won't let us talk to him. They got a lawyer, so now we've got to do everything through him."

"His dad's a lawyer," I point out. "Why do they need anyone else?"

"I guess they just want to be extra cautious."

"Because they're covering something up?"

Captain Talarico shrugs demonstratively. "You know as much as I do. Kaitlyn, if it were just your sister missing, then yeah, Neil's a good suspect. But do you really think that kid killed both girls? I mean, that's the kind of psycho crap that people don't usually get into until they're in their twenties or thirties."

"I have no idea," I say, shaking my head. "But the two cases have to be connected, right? I mean, what are the chances? You know as well as I do that we cops don't like to believe in coincidences."

"They disappeared under similar circumstances, but Natalie turned up dead. Maybe some drifter got one and another one got killed by someone close to her."

He's talking out loud, but I can't help but cringe at the thought of some drifter attacking my little sister.

"I'm sorry. I didn't mean to say that."

"No, it's fine. I understand," I mumble. "I want you to talk to me like a colleague. I insist. I need to know the truth."

"The truth is that we got nothing," he says, rubbing his stomach, and then giving off a little burp, followed by an apology.

"God, in the afternoons, I get the worst heartburn," he says.

"You've got to see a doctor about that. It could be an ulcer."

"Yeah, or something worse. I hate doctors."

I follow him back to his office, where he pops a couple of Tums in his mouth.

"How's your mother holding up?" the captain asks, pointing to the flimsy plastic chair in the corner where I can take a seat. I bring it over to the desk.

"She's doing good. I actually found out that she's sort of involved with someone who used to work here."

"Oh, yeah?"

"Danny Weidner."

"Oh, yeah, of course." He smiles. "Good cop. He retired a few years ago, or was it five? It's been a while."

Captain Talarico looks up, again thinking out loud.

"Apparently they met in some support group and I had no idea that they were together until today."

"Yeah, I'm sure she had a good reason to keep it from you."

"Because I'm kind of an ass?" I ask, tilting my head to one side.

"You? You're nothing but sunshine."

He smiles.

We banter back and forth and I look around his office. There are knickknacks from home and pictures of various trips. Unlike Captain Medvil's office back home, which is rather sterile and empty, Captain Talarico's office is warm and inviting.

He spots me looking at a picture of a young woman in an elegant black gown.

"That's my oldest at prom. Now she's in college, studying to be a speech therapist. I still can't believe it. Time just flies by."

"I guess so." I nod, always finding that it's an odd statement that everyone seems to make.

I haven't had that experience with time, but then again, I've never seen my own child grow up. My relationship with my sister has always been a little complicated and I've sometimes wondered what it'd be like to raise a child on my own.

"So, you and Luke Gavinson. How's that going?" I'm taken a little aback by his statement. "I know you two think that you're hiding it, but we all know the truth."

"Great," I say with a tinge of sarcasm.

"Look, you're not really doing anything improper. He works for a different law enforcement agency, but he is investigating your sister's disappearance."

"Well, not anymore. Not since the case kind of went cold."

"It's not official yet," Captain Talarico says.

"How about between friends?" I lean forward.

"Between friends, I'd say that we got nothing. Whoever did this is an expert. I don't know if he has prior experience, but I have my suspicions."

I don't want to talk about this anymore, so I ask him about my dad. "Was he an informant?"

"Yeah, he was." He nods.

"I didn't know that. Why didn't anyone tell me?"

"I thought that you knew," he says quietly. "And then with all of this business with your sister, I didn't think it was appropriate to bring it up."

"So this JD Ryder, what was his relationship to my dad?"

"He was your dad's handler. Hal ran the biggest bookie business up in the San Bernardino mountains. People from down in the valley even came up here when they couldn't get games. He lent a lot of people money and took a lot of bets. The only reason why he was protected was because he told the cops about a lot of dealings that were going on."

"I just can't believe that he would do that."

"You prefer that he didn't?" the captain asks.

"No, I mean, obviously, I'm for fighting crime, as you know, but I just had no idea that my dad was so corrupt."

"He wasn't corrupt." The captain shakes his head. "He was a survivor. He was facing years behind bars for a robbery. He made a deal with the prosecution. He wanted to be there to watch you grow up. And then when your sister was born, he wanted to be there for her, too."

"So, what do you think happened to him?" I ask.

"Are you trying to say you don't believe the suicide theory?" Captain Talarico narrows his eyes.

"I don't know what to believe."

"I don't know either, to tell you the truth. Your father had a lot of issues. He had a bit of a drug problem. He had a lot of bad people after him. But he and JD were very close. If anyone were to know what happened, he'd know."

"How do I get in touch with him?" I ask.

"He lives in a cabin out in Fawnskin. He usually goes fishing every morning. He likes to follow the same schedule and do the same thing, so he shouldn't be too hard to find."

"Okay." I nod. "Thank you for your help."

"When you find him, you tell him hello. Tell him don't be a stranger and that we miss him," Captain Talarico says and gives me a wink.

22

One thing is for sure: JD Ryder is not a hard man to find. I look up the address that Captain Talarico gave me on Google Maps, and when I drive up to his small cabin up in the hills above the lake, I see him coming back carrying a cooler and his fishing rod.

He's a slight man dressed in a flannel shirt, a thick head of hair as white as the snow. He has a nice tan, probably from being out in the sun.

"So, you are the elusive Kaitlyn Carr," he says with a big smile. I extend my hand and he pulls me in for a big bear hug. "I can't tell you how great it is to meet you."

JD's reaction to seeing me takes me by surprise. I thought I would have to fight a battle to get him to say a word, but he looks genuinely happy that I came to see him.

"Well, how are you doing? What have you been up to?" he asks. "I know that you work for the LAPD."

"Yeah, I do. I'm a detective," I say.

"Wow. I always knew that you'd do something special with your life." "Look, I feel a little bit awkward here, but do we know each other well? I mean, I wasn't certain that you would even know my name."

"You're Hal's daughter. He talked about you often. We met a few times, but you were a kid. Not sure you would've remembered."

“Captain Talarico told me that you were his handler."

"Yes, he worked with me," he says. "Our relationship started out professional, but then we discovered that we had a lot in common and became friends."

"But he was still reporting on others, right?" I ask, trying to choose my words carefully.

"Yes. He was an informant," JD says without being as tactful. "And we worked together for many years. That was part of his plea deal. That's why he didn't go away for that robbery. You know how that works.”

He gives me a wink.

"Yes, of course. I'm very familiar with plea deals. I'm just a little bit confused about some aspects of your relationship."

"Why don't you come in? Let's have a chat," JD says, nudging me toward the front door of his cabin.

It's a small, two-bedroom, but I'd be surprised if it was more than 700-square feet. And he tells me that it was one of the cabins that was built by the National Forest Service that he bought almost twenty years ago.

"My wife and I got divorced. I wanted her to have the house, have a good place for the kids to live, and this was affordable. I don't need much."

“So, your kids still live around here?" I ask.

"No, LA, Sacramento. One's a lawyer, the other's a teacher."

The cabin is sparsely decorated, all wood inside with a big fireplace in one corner. He grabs a set of mismatched mugs and offers to pour me some coffee, but taking one look at the pot with its stale remains from at least a couple of days ago, I pass.

"Don't you usually go fishing in the morning? Isn't that the best time?" I ask.

"Yeah, but I'm not much of a fisherman, and I don't like waking up that early. I like being on the water in my boat, and I just hang the rod out there and see if anything's going to take a bite."

We talk about the weather, nothing in particular, for a little bit, and I catch him up on my career, which he seems very interested in. He finishes one cup of coffee and follows it up with another. When he brings out an assortment of baked goods from the pantry, I can't say no.

I ask JD more about my father when the timing seems right, and I eat about half of my Biscotti.

"So, were you really friends with my dad?"

"Real good friends. He saved my butt a few times; he even heard that some guys out of San Bernardino weren't too happy with a recent arrest that I'd made and they put out a contract on my head."

"You know, I'm glad that he was helpful, but it makes me concerned. People like that usually don't do well in society."

"Yeah, I know. Of course." He smirks. "He worked for the cops."

"Do you think he was trying to make good? I mean, what was his motivation?"

"Initially, he had no choice. It wasn't some do-gooder thing. He was facing a lot of time and he needed to find a way to stay with his family. But, as we developed a bit of a relationship and became friends, and I don't use that word lightly, I realized that he was looking for a way out, out of the game."

"Was he still selling drugs?"

"He really cut back on that. No more schools, no more shady operations. At least not the way it was before. He tried to focus more on gambling and taking bets, but you know how it is. It doesn't always work out."

"No, I don't know how it is." I shake my head.

"Well, you want what's best, but then things kind of go awry."

Darkness seems to settle over him. The expression on his face changes, so does his demeanor and it becomes a little off.

I wait for him to continue, but he doesn't. He's going to ask me to say this out loud. I don't particularly want to, but if I want answers, this is the only way to go.

"What do you think about what happened to him?" I ask.

"You're here to ask if he committed suicide?"

I nod.

"It's hard for me to tell. It seems plausible."

"But you don't think so?"

"He talked about it often," JD says, after a long pause. "He made me promise not to tell anyone, not his family. Meaning, not you, not Violet, not your mom, but I knew that you were going to have questions with answers that only he could give you."

"Do you think somebody came after him? I mean, he turned state's evidence on so many bad people, maybe one of them killed him, staged it to look like a suicide?"

JD takes a deep breath in and exhales, letting his shoulders fall.

"You don't think so? I mean, how could it not be that?" I ask.

"It's very plausible, of course, and I would probably think the same thing that you are thinking right now, but I knew Hal."

I open my mouth to say something else, but JD cuts me off.

"I also have the letter that he left for whoever came asking questions."

My eyes dart from side to side.

What questions? What is he talking about?

I sit back in the overly soft chair that feels like it's pushing me back into itself as I struggle to get out. JD walks over to his antique desk and pulls out the top drawer. As he rifles around, I feel my blood pressure dropping and my hands turning to ice.

The letter is weathered, worn, but unopened. He hands it to me.

It has the last name Carr on it.

"I don't know what the letter says," JD insists. "But a couple of days before it happened, he handed it to me and he said to give it to either you, his wife, or your little sister after she got older, and it would contain the answers that you were looking for."

I want to rip into it, open it as quickly as I can, but I feel the need to linger.

"You don't have to tell me what it says. I know you want to read it. You're here. I did my bit. It was nice to see you and I'm glad you're doing well."

Remaining largely speechless, I walk out the door, holding onto the only thing that can provide me with answers but knowing full well that it may not have any at all.

23

I grasp onto the letter and cradle it in my hands as I make my way down to my car. I rip into it without even turning on the engine or bothering with heating the car up. I've waited long enough and I just can't wait any longer. In neat capital letters, I spot my name at the top.

My darling loves,

I don't know which one of you will be the one to read this, and I don't want to make any guesses. I know that you will only come to talk to JD once you have questions that you can't possibly have answered anywhere else. I want you to know that I love you all very much and you're the reason why my life was so full of the happiness that it was. I have made a lot of mistakes and I have a lot of regrets but sharing my life with you is not one of them. If you are reading this letter, that means that my body was found and you are uncertain as to whether or not I have committed suicide or if someone had me killed. I want you to believe me when I say that I died by my own hand. I did it.

My cycles of depression and sadness have become unbearable. I can no longer see a way out, and when I was diagnosed with early onset Parkinson's, I knew that things were just going to get worse.

I was going to forget more and more memories and the dark periods were going to last longer. I didn't want any of that. I wanted to remember you all.

I wanted you to remember me as I was. I have been an informant with the sheriff's department for many years, and through my time there, I've made a number of friends. JD was one of the closest and I trusted him more than I ever trusted anyone else. I trusted him with my life and that's why you are reading this now.

I know that you have questions and you probably will have them for a long time. I don't know yet how I'm going to do it, but I know that I'm in a happy place right now, and I'm trying to savor every moment.

I'm sorry that I will not see Kaitlyn become the strong, assertive, beautiful woman that I know that she will be and I will not be here to see Violet grow up, but I'm thankful for the time that I've had with both of my girls and with you, darling, the love of my life.

I read the words with tears streaming down my face. I miss him terribly and holding this letter in my hands makes me feel like he's right here, whispering the words into my ear.

I hope you take care of my girls, darling, he writes and I continue to cry knowing that the letter is really addressed to my mom, but she wasn't the one who read it.

I also know deep down that you know what I'm going through and how hard it has been for me through all of these periods of darkness.

I want to be with you while I'm still here and I want you to remember me for who I was, not the man that I will become once this disease takes hold of me.

I'm sorry if you have any doubts as to who took my life. And though there are many people after me, I have always been my own worst enemy. Take care of each other.

Love forever,

Hal/ Dad

Two days later, I find myself back in Los Angeles in Luke's arms. He has a few days off and we spend every moment together. We order Chinese food and let the containers pile up on the coffee table, as we watch mindless television and show each other ridiculous stories on Reddit and YouTube. He's partial to watching channels where people play video games, and I love reruns of *Dragons' Den* and *Shark Tank*, as well as any crime documentary or show that I can get my hands on.

We talk about my dad a little bit, and the fact that my mom kept his early onset Parkinson's diagnosis from me. He told her about it, but she wasn't sure until I showed her the letter. I asked her why she never told me and she said that she wanted me to remember him as he was.

I guess I'll never understand why my mom does the things that she does. I admit this to Luke and he says that's likely the case with lots of kids and parents. You just don't get where they're coming from and that's just how it is.

That night after we make love, Luke holds me in his arms for a long time and tells me that he loves me.

"Let's get married," he whispers into my ear. "Let's have a little ceremony. If you don't want to invite your mom, you don't have to."

He chuckles and I do, too.

"I don't think that I want a big dress or a big party or anything like that," I admit.

"That's fine. I just want you to be my wife." He kisses the top of my head.

We talk about Sydney and their shotgun wedding. We visited them yesterday and they all seem to be doing well. The baby's getting stronger every day and I hope she gets to go home soon.

"What's wrong?" Luke pulls away for a moment, noticing that something in my face has changed. We have a little flameless candle on for mood lighting, and I watch the way it dances off his face.

"I want to marry you. I do. I just... I don't know, with my sister still missing. It's like I want a resolution before I move on with my life. Whatever that resolution may be."

"I totally understand," he says, propping his head up with his hand.

Still, I can see the sadness in his eyes. I'm sad, too. The problem with my sister's disappearance is that there's no guarantee there will ever be answers. He knows this as well as I do, but neither of us say it out loud; not quite yet.

"I'm not saying that I never want to marry you or that I'm going to make you wait forever."

I reach over and intertwine my fingers with his. "It's just that right now, I feel like I have to wait."

"Do you still think... Do you think that she's out there?" he asks.

"I don't know. I want to believe she is."

My next day at work, I get down to reviewing Kelly Flynn's file. Once and for all, I have to get to the bottom of this. So far, both Sonny, her ex-husband, and Logan, the guy that she went on two dates with, have been successful at avoiding me but I'm going to change that today.

When I meet with Captain Medvil and give him a brief update, he stresses that it is absolutely unacceptable that the case is still unsolved.

"You have to bring them in. You have to question them. One of them did it. You know it and so do I."

This is also the same person who was so sure of the fact that Jesus' Gutierrez was the one responsible for her murder.

"Of course, it had to be him." I can practically hear his words ring in my ears. "She was seen almost getting into his car."

I don't bring this up. He's right. I haven't made the Flynn case a priority, but from now on, it's going to be.

24

Later that afternoon, I get some good news. They found a few loose strands of hair on Kelly's body and the DNA was matched to a man by the name of Christian Bertrand, with a long record of robbery, assault, drugs, and an assortment of other things. When I look through his file, I see that he is a low-level guy in the motorcycle club, the Nighthawks.

I check him out online and, of course, he has a well filled out Facebook account and Instagram page promoting the Nighthawks in all of its glory. If he has any plans to rise further in the organization, he's going to have to delete all that stuff, but for now, he's just proud to be there.

I update Medvil on what I've found and tell him that I'm on my way to talk to Christian.

"How are you thinking about approaching this?" he asks without looking away from his computer screen.

I know that he's knee deep in all of the political fallout from what Thomas has done, with lots of interview requests from various news outlets, not just in the Los Angeles and Southern California region, but all over the world. To say that Medvil is not a happy camper would be a huge understatement.

"I was going to go out to his place and feel it out for a little bit," I say.

"Do you really think he's going to talk?"

"I don't know. He posts a lot on Instagram, a lot of things that the club probably isn't too happy about. He's walking a fine line between giving the Nighthawks PR and getting them the wrong kind of attention. Maybe he's stupid enough to talk to me."

"Well, be friendly. Take it easy. Try to get him to say something," he advises, as if anything like that needs to be said.

An hour later, I find Christian at his apartment on Figueroa. I show my badge, but he doesn't even flinch. He's used to the cops coming around, asking questions.

He's a tall guy with long hair going all the way down his back, broad shoulders, thick, beefy arms, and tattoos that cover about ninety percent of his visible skin except for the face. He's wearing a short sleeve, nondescript black t-shirt and low hanging jeans, and he doesn't look like he's a stranger to the gym.

Even though he invites me in, I opt to stay in the doorway, feeling a little bit apprehensive at being alone in an apartment with a guy with that much of a record. I invite him over to the station, but of course, he passes on the invitation, saying that he's too busy.

"Have you ever met Kelly Flynn?" I jump right in but withhold the information about the hairs and the DNA to myself for now.

"Well, I know that she was killed and she was Sonny's ex-wife. It's really tragic what happened," he says, leaning on the doorway, crossing his big biceps in front of him.

There's a phone in his hand that he holds with the screen facing down and it rings and vibrates incessantly as we talk, but he doesn't look at it once.

"You don't need to get that?" I ask, slightly annoyed.

"No, they'll wait," Christian says without breaking eye contact.

He's intimidating me, hovering over me. It was a good decision to stay out of his apartment, and I broaden my shoulders and widen my stance to show him that he's got nothing on me. The problem is that it's nothing but bravado.

"Do you know how she was killed?" I ask.

"Yeah, I heard it all over the news."

"Did Sonny say anything?" I jump ahead, the words escaping my lips.

I bite the inside of my cheek to remind myself to keep this conversation moving smoothly.

That's the first rule of asking questions. You cannot interrupt the person who's speaking just in case they say a little bit more than they want to. "Sorry about that," I backtrack. "You were saying? You know about what happened to her?"

"Everyone does. They play it on loop on the news because she's a pretty blonde woman and has a kid. I know how these things work."

"What was your reaction when you heard about the murder?"

"Well, I was very surprised. I mean, she seemed like a nice gal, friendly. I know that she had a lot of issues with Sonny, but he was really distraught. A bullet to the back of the head? I mean, nobody wants that for their kid's mother."

I lean a little bit closer, examining his face, but he remains stoic.

"Look, I have to get to work."

“Where’s that?"

"Amazon warehouse in Commerce. My shift's starting in an hour and with traffic, you know how it is."

I nod. I ask him a few more questions about his relationship with Sonny, but he just shrugs it off.

"I'm in the club, but I'm not privy to anything. It's just a loose organization of bikers. We do a lot of fundraising, that kind of thing."

"Oh, really?" I ask, tilting my head. "So, no selling drugs for the cartels, nothing of that sort?"

This doesn't faze him. He gives me a little smirk. "Of course not. We’re just motorcycle enthusiasts. You know that."

I walk out with him knowing that there's no way that I’ll get anything else from him if I don’t give him a glimpse of my hand.

He heads toward a Buick SUV six-seater in pearl white, an unusual car for someone like him to drive.

"It's my girlfriend's," he says, reading my mind. "She's got three kids, all of their sports crap and a very complicated custody arrangement. You got anymore questions?"

I clear my throat. "You said that you have never met Kelly."

"Yeah."

I shift my weight from one foot to the other, fighting back the pinching that these brand-new dress shoes are doing to my toes.

"You told me that you never met Kelly, right?" I repeat myself.

"Well, no, not exactly. I mean, I've seen her around, but that's about it."

"Around where?" I ask.

"The clubhouse. Sonny's place. Whenever she would drop off the kid, there would always be some sort of incident, either with Sonny or his mother."

This statement makes it harder for me to put him in the corner, but I try anyway.

"So, would you happen to have any idea why strands of your hair were found on her body?"

"What?" Christian asks, breaking his serious demeanor for a moment.

The blood seems to rush from his face, turning his skin a translucent blue color, but only momentarily, as he regains his composure.

"Well, I have no idea." He hesitates, moving his weight from one foot to another. His nervousness slides to the surface.

He's having doubts about my case. He knows that I have my eye on him and I'm not just here asking questions in an exploratory manner.

"I don't know," Christian says after a pause that's way too long. "I don't even know if what you're saying is true."

He challenges me, narrowing his eyes.

"Oh, it is true. We found your DNA evidence on her. Hairs to be exact. The medical examiner's doing a review of the case, seeing if perhaps there's something else we missed."

"More like planting evidence," Christian interjects. "I know what the LAPD is all about."

This takes me aback. For a moment, I had forgotten that he's no stranger to law enforcement. Someone else in his position might admit to something, might try to explain something away, but he has served time. He knows how the legal system works, and he knows that staying quiet and keeping your mouth shut is the best way to go ninety percent of the time.

"Listen, I have to go to work. Unless, of course, you're arresting me."

Christian waits for me to respond and I'm forced to shake my head no.

"Okay. I'll see you around."

Watching him drive away, I want to kick myself for how I handled this interrogation.

It could have gone better. It should have. But I needed to see his reaction. The hairs do belong to him.

The LAPD may be responsible for framing others, and have a history of doing less than upright police work, but in this particular case, I'm onto something.

He had something to do with her murder, and I'm going to find out what it is.

25

Instead of returning to the office, I decide to follow Christian Bertrand to his place of work. I have the location in my file since it's part of his parole conditions. I spot his car outside the Amazon warehouse in the parking lot and stop by 7-Eleven for a crappy cup of coffee and a delicious pack of M&Ms to squash my hunger.

When I roll down the window, I hear a few people outside the warehouse talking, mentioning twelve-hour shifts. I go through my files on the computer and do a little work while I wait. The employees take their smoking breaks in the designated smoking area not too far from where I park, and luckily, I'm in my Prius, not a police-issued car. It's a lot less noticeable this way.

A mere two hours later, which is hardly any time at all for a stakeout, Christian emerges and inhales two cigarettes. Just as he's about to go back in without talking to anyone but scrolling through his phone, a woman in a tight-fitting dress, high heels, and ridiculously long nails, approaches him and starts pounding the side of his head.

To get a better look, I lean over the steering wheel almost honking the horn, but luckily, catch myself in time.

Rolling down the window, I hear her screaming at him and calling him all sorts of curse words for cheating on her, something I quickly figure out is the main problem. Christian gaslights her for a while, telling her that he has no idea what she's talking about, that the text messages to the other woman do not belong to him and he did not send them.

Their voices are so elevated that I can hear every single thing with incredible clarity.

"Look, Amelia. I got to get back to work. My break is only ten minutes, you know that. I'm going to get fired, and then we're going to have bigger issues. We'll talk about this when I get back."

"Oh, hell no! I'm not going to be there, and neither will any of your stuff."

"You better take that back," he snaps, pointing his finger in her face. "Or you know what this fist is going to do."

She continues to punch at the side of his head, but since he's almost double her size he grabs hold of her and pulls her aside, not exactly calming the situation, but at least deescalating it.

He physically peels her fingers off the side of his forearms and then escapes inside the warehouse, leaving her fuming outside. I debate for a moment whether I should approach her. No, not yet.

She's still red in the face, pissed off, angry for catching him in the act of cheating. But that doesn't mean she's going to talk to the cops.

I get back to my phone and start to furiously look through Christian's Instagram page. Scrolling down a little bit, I see a picture of a butt in tight leather pants, tagged with Amelia Ringwold.

"That's her. That's her," I say out loud, finding a treasure trove of stealthy shots, closeups of her round booty, and links to her page, as well as her OnlyFans account.

The little engagement ring emoji on her profile with Christian Bertrand's handle right after it says it all. Their wedding is planned for June of next year.

When I get back to work, I uncover her real identity, Sarah Thompson, along with a long slew of minor crimes and misdemeanors: unpaid parking tickets, theft, and even trespassing at a plastic surgery clinic.

She's not hard to find because she's linked to the motorcycle club, which has the names of everyone who's part of the organization, as well as many of the women that help them get their business done.

We figured out long ago that the women involved in these organizations really do help in prosecuting these guys. Same goes for gang units. The men cheat, the men lie, and their girlfriends and wives at some point stop covering for them and can occasionally be flipped to talk. I wonder whether this Amelia Ringwold, or rather, Sarah Thompson, is someone who is sufficiently angry at this point to say something about her beloved. Or maybe I should let her stew on it for a little bit longer prior to addressing her.

Her address is the same as Christian's, and while he works the night shift, I sit outside their apartment building and wait. Maybe tonight will be the night that she goes out. At nine thirty, just an hour and a half into my stakeout, I see her dressed in casual jeans and a loose-fitting top heading outside the apartment building and across the street to a bar. I turn, grab my keys and my phone, and follow her.

26

The bar is dark and dingy and has a definite dive bar quality. The kind of place I would seek out when I was at USC, wanting to go somewhere cool only to find out that other college kids have already discovered it.

This one has a mixed bag of clientele. Twenty- and thirty-somethings and a few old timers, but it's not filled entirely with the retired drowning their sorrows in alcohol.

Not at all.

This is the kind of place you could be alone if you wanted to, but not somewhere you would stand out if you are a first timer.

I take a seat a few empty bar stools away from Amelia, and I glance over to her after I order my Old

Fashioned. This isn't a typical drink for me, but it seems like an old-fashioned kind of bar.

Amelia looks completely different. Gone are the five-inch heels, the skintight dress, even the eyelashes. The only thing that remains of the woman I saw earlier are the long nails: aggressively pointy at the tips and the kind that would make most daily tasks impossible. Luckily, no one chats her up and everyone seems busy with their own group of friends.

"I like your nails," I say, after carefully debating the kind of compliment that I should pay her in order to open our conversation up for discussion. I don't want her to feel like I'm coming on to her or anything like that. But, more like a girl looking for some girl talk after a hard day at work.

"Thanks." She taps them on the counter.

A woman in her fifties with a scowling expression on her face shakes her head slightly, just out of my view.

"They're kind of a pain, as you can imagine."

"Yeah. I've never had ones that long."

She glances at mine: short stubbly ones. There's no manicure in sight but she doesn't comment.

"Guys seem to like them." She rolls her eyes. "But then again, they like all sorts of stuff that's complicated and unwieldy and kind of annoying, like lashes and tight clothes, don't they?"

I nod in agreement.

"God, I'm so sick of men," she continues.

I can tell that she has a lot to get off her chest and I hope she opens up to me. I know that I have to find the right time to introduce myself as a police officer, but for now, I'll just bide my time, get a little bit friendlier, get her to trust me more.

"Dealing with someone in particular?" I ask.

"I'll have what she's having," Amelia tells the bartender. When the drink arrives, she takes a gulp and then spits it out.

"Oh my God, how can you drink this? This is terrible."

"Eh, sometimes I feel like a little whiskey," I say. "When the day gets hard."

"No, I'll have a Lemon Drop."

After a long pause, she says, "Just found out my fiancé is a piece of crap. Got this girl pregnant."

"Wow. Really?"

"I mean, I knew he had a wandering eye, but not to that degree. Seriously. I'm just so pissed off."

"I'm really sorry," I say and ask her more.

She tells me that they met four months ago, started dating, which she thought was exclusively. But, then one day she came home from work and found some girl's underwear in her bed.

"Under my pillow, can you believe that? Used. Pink panties. He cried. He told me a million I'm sorrys and I was such a fool, I believed him. One of these days I have to tell myself just because the guy's hot and he's got a nice body on him, doesn't mean I have to believe every single thing that he says. If I were smart, I'd date some accountant with a pudgy belly and a receding hairline, then he'd know my worth."

"Why don't you?" I ask.

"I don't know. I guess I'm an addict."

"Addict?"

"No. No drugs or anything like that. I stay away from all that. But I am a sex addict," she says. "It's stupid and I should probably go talk to someone, but this guy I was telling you about, he had me open an OnlyFans account. You know what that is?"

I nod.

"Yeah. You know what that is." Amelia smiles and I feel myself blushing.

It's a website that blew up recently that allows people to post themselves dancing, performing sexual activities, single, or with others.

“I did a little porn back in the day back when you needed someone to hold the camera, that kind of world. But, this was a whole new thing. You just put your phone on the tripod, smile, take off your clothes. I’ve never made easier money."

"I've heard of it.” I nod. “There were a bunch of articles in Forbes.”

"Yeah, I guess. Well, my boyfriend introduced me to it and I couldn't resist."

"So, is that what you're doing now?" I ask.

"Yeah, totally. I mean, that's why I got this whole getup with the nails. I don't like to wear this kind of stuff, but it’s part of the show. He paid for my wigs, clothes, everything.”

"So, he was what? Your pimp?"

"I guess you could say that, but he makes way too much money doing what he does to take any money from me. He just helped me out. It was good for a while. And I got to have lots of sex, not so much with him on camera, but myself, some girls, that kind of thing. It worked out for a while. But, now this…"

"Well, if it's…" Amelia kind of stops talking and lets her thoughts drift off.

"Sorry, I don't mean to be dominating this conversation." She finishes her Lemon Drop and gets another.

"No problem," I say with a casual shrug. "I'm just here for a little drink and some friendly conversation."

"I like that." Amelia nods.

27

Amelia continues to talk on and on, complaining about her boyfriend and venting as if we're old friends. I like that I make her feel so comfortable. Still, I keep looking for an in.

"So, what is it that your boyfriend does?"

"You mean soon-to-be ex-boyfriend?" She laughs, tossing her hair. "He's in this motorcycle club, thinks that he's the shit, like a big-time drug dealer or something."

"Oh, really?"

"Yeah, totally. I mean, he's been with them for a little while. I don't know exactly what they do, but it's nothing good."

I finish two drinks, and she does three, and the conversation meanders. But she offers me nothing in particular. Then just as I'm about to ask again, Christian walks into the bar and sees us.

"What are you doing talking to *her*?" He rushes up to Amelia, pointing his finger in my face.

"I thought you were working late," she starts to say. "What are you doing here?"

He approaches me aggressively but doesn't touch. I get up from my bar stool.

"Do you know who she is?" he asks Amelia. She shakes her head no. "She's a cop. What did you tell her?"

"A cop?" Amelia gasps.

"What did you tell her?" he yells, and everyone looks up. The secret's out. I can try to dial it in, try to take it back. Instead, I reach into my back pocket and hand Amelia my card. He grabs it out of her hand, but she pushes away from him and picks it up off the floor.

"You're a detective with the LAPD?" she says, her mouth dropping open."I didn’t mean anything I said."

"You're not doing anything illegal," I say. Her body starts to shake.

"What did you tell her?" Christian yells.

"You put your hands on her and I'm going to arrest you," I say calmly.

A manager comes up to us and asks us to leave.

"Come on, let's get out of here."

Christian pulls on Amelia's arm and she looks stunned. Turning to face me, she shakes her head.

"I was just joking about everything," she says, probably going over every statement she'd made in her mind, trying to think if she'd mentioned anything illegal.

"I'm here if you want to talk. I'm not going to arrest you," I say.

"Do you know why she's here?" Christian yells, pulling her out the front door. I follow quickly behind them.

"She's trying to frame me for that girl's murder."

"We didn't even talk about that," Amelia says, furrowing her brows.

I lick my lips.

"Tell him we didn't even talk about that," she begs me.

"She's right," I say.

"You're trying to tell me that you were here just by coincidence?" Christian laughs. "I know how you operate. You're the LAPD. You know how many innocent people are behind bars because of *you*? I'm not going to be one of them."

He tugs on Amelia's arm, pulling her across the street. She turns back to look at me a couple of times and then I see her slip my card in her back pocket and I say a silent prayer, hoping that maybe she'll give me a call.

THAT EVENING I return home with a heavy heart, wondering if I could have handled that better. Maybe if I had just come forward and told her the truth, she would have opened up more. She was already angry with Christian, but I let the charade go on.

The problem is that it's hard to tell which is the best way to go. I just have to take a chance. With some people, it's better to play games. With others, it's better to be straightforward and honest. Amelia didn't give me much, but whatever goodwill I'd built up had disappeared as soon as Christian called me out and told her who I really was.

What was he doing there anyway? He was supposed to be working the full shift. Did he get fired? I wonder.

My thoughts get all swirled together, and my head starts to pound. Not many people know that I'm an introvert. That means I need some time off from people once in a while in order to regain energy.

I'm not necessarily shy, though I used to be, but I do need my alone time. It's like I have this battery that gets drained every time I'm in a social situation, and it needs to be built back up. But just being home under the covers, lying down, doing nothing in particular, goes a long way to help me recharge.

Luke's not home when I get here, and I climb directly into bed after a quick shower. I put on Amazon Prime and start it. The quiet time and the mindless television allows me to drift off to sleep. The next thing I know I wake up in the middle of the night with a pounding headache. A couple of Excedrin do a bit to help, but the migraine comes on strong.

The following day, despite the fact that I need to talk to Sonny and Christian again, I decide to follow Logan instead. Since we found the strands of hair belonging to Christian, I've pretty much written Logan off as a suspect.

I wonder if maybe he still has something important to add to the overall conversation. I haven't had a chance to talk to him. At his apartment building, I watch him head to his car and decide to follow. Ten minutes later, he pulls into the cemetery. I park nearby just out of sight and watch him walk over the hill.

I haven't been here before but as I follow him up the walkway, I see the gray stone in the distance. I give him a few minutes of quiet time. Just as he's about to leave, I approach him.

There are tears in his eyes that he quickly wipes away with the back of his hand. It's a sunny, beautiful, cloudless day in Los Angeles. Kelly Flynn has a small gravestone marking her name, date of birth, the date that her body was found, and the words *beloved mother* underneath.

"Are you following me?" Logan asks.

"I was just coming to talk to you," I say, and he doesn't push it any further. "I miss her," he whispers. "Did you find out who did this?"

"No, not yet. I just wanted to talk to you a little bit more about it."

He shakes his head no.

Dressed in a casual t-shirt and board shorts, Logan's tan skin glistens in the light, and his long blonde hair falls into his eyes. He's wearing a pair of sunglasses, which he plops down over his face, probably in an effort to cover his tears.

"Did you get her those flowers?" I ask, pointing to the daisies on the grave. He nods.

"We only had a few dates. But I felt like we'd known each other for a long time, like she was this friend, and confidant, and a woman who I could spend the rest of my life with."

"I wanted to talk to you about someone named Christian Bertrand. Have you ever heard that name before?"

"No," he says. "Who is that?"

"Somebody who works with her ex-husband, who is in his motorcycle club."

"Is that who you think did it?"

"We found some evidence that points to him. I'm not exactly sure."

"I've never heard that name." Logan shakes his head. "But I'm sure that her ex-husband was involved. He really wanted to get custody of their son, and he just seemed really controlling. They had a long history. She told me that he hit her. That's why she was leaving. She just didn't want to put up with that anymore, and she didn't want her son seeing him treat her like that."

Suddenly, Logan breaks down and begins to sob. He crouches down and buries his head in his arms. I feel awkward standing on the hill next to him. I lean over and touch him slightly on the shoulder, but he pushes me away. I let him cry for a few moments then he sucks it all in, wipes his face, and pulls his Ray-Bans to the top of his head.

I ask him more questions, like the ones I asked before and his answers match his previous ones. That's what we look for in interrogations. Do people repeat what they said word for word? Or do they vary it just a little, but not so much that they forget what they said earlier? Logan continues to fall on my list of suspects.

Initially, I was torn between whether Sonny or Logan was responsible for Kelly's death, but now my focus is almost exclusively on Sonny, especially given Christian's DNA evidence and his connection to the Nighthawks. The problem is that Christian doesn't have much motive, and unless he confesses and turns state's evidence on his boss, which seems unlikely, I don't have much of a case. A few strands of hair are not enough. The district attorney will want more, especially to make a case for an execution-style hit.

Christian doesn't have a motive, but Sonny does.

Talking to Logan and seeing his heartbreak for a woman that he had essentially only met a few times and has only been on a few dates with, makes my feel for him.

He looks lost, like a sad little puppy. I know that he's been through a lot in his life. He has suffered.

Meeting Kelly was a positive thing, something that he thought maybe would change his luck. It didn't.

"You really need to find out who did this," he says, taking a step closer. "That son of a bitch has to pay for everything that he has done. She did not deserve that. She deserved happiness, and love, and just all the beauty in the world, because that's what she was."

Logan's face splinters from the pain.

"Promise me that you'll find out who did this, and you'll make them pay," he says, fighting back tears.

"I promise," I whisper.

28

For a couple of days, I toil filling out paperwork, working on other cases, and mainly just thinking about what happened to Kelly, but not how I can prove who had killed her.

When an unfamiliar number rings, I'm tempted to let it go to voice mail but since this is my work phone, I answer. As soon as I hear her voice, I say a silent prayer of thanks for the fact that I did.

It's Amelia Ringwold, real name, Sarah Thompson. She's crying. She gives me the address of a bus stop on Figueroa Street where I can pick her up. And I get there in less than ten minutes by hitting all green lights and driving twenty miles above the speed limit. She's sitting on a bench, her head hanging low, big Jackie Onassis sunglasses shielding her face.

I park at an empty meter, half a block away.

She doesn't see me walking up to her until I sit down on the bench.

"Are you okay?" I ask.

"No," she mumbles.

The left part of her face is covered in big bruises with lacerations along her jawline. Black and blue indentations, like someone had put a fist through her face multiple times. Her nose is broken.

I ask her to remove her sunglasses because it must be incredibly painful to keep them on over her broken face.

At first, she shakes her head no. A few minutes later, she gives in.

"Oh my God! What happened?" I ask, breathless at the sight. Her eyes are two thin slits, puffy and deformed.

She reaches for her sunglasses, but I stop her.

"Let me take you to the hospital."

"No," Amelia says sternly, wincing with pain.

“Please! Your nose is probably broken. So, is your jaw."

"No, I can't. He'll know. They'll make me file a police report."

"You're talking to a cop right now."

"I know. But I'm hoping that you can keep it between us."

"I can't," I say. "I'm a mandatory reporter."

"I'm not going to press charges against him."

"You're not?"

"No. He'll do something worse."

"Worse than *this*?"

"I'm alive, right? I'm talking to you."

"Okay. Let's do that. Do you want to get in my car? We can get some coffee."

That sounds appealing to her.

"When was the last time that you ate?" I ask.

"I don't know. Yesterday?"

"Let me take you to a diner."

"No. I can't be seen in public like this. It's just awful."

When she starts to get up, I can see that the bruising goes way farther than her face. Amelia holds onto her ribs. And I wonder whether he slammed her against the wall or into a table.

"How about I get you some food? What's your favorite?"

"In-N-Out," she whispers.

"Okay. Let's do that. We can sit in my car and we can talk."

"Okay."

I go through the drive-thru, order her a burger, animal style, and a large, fresh-cut fries. I'm not particularly hungry so I opt for a Sprite and an order of fries. She seems to relax a little bit in the front seat of my Prius.

I debated whether to take the patrol car here but I didn't want to draw too much attention to her in case any of the neighbors were watching.

"Why were you waiting for me at that bus stop?" I ask.

"Because Christian got drunk, fell asleep, and I snuck out. I wasn't sure if you were going to put on your lights or come in your cop car. But I didn't want to risk it, you know?"

"Yeah. I understand."

Again, I give thanks for the fact that we were on the same wavelength.

"The bus stop was as far as I got before I couldn't walk anymore. It was just too much."

"No. I get it," I say. "I'm glad you called me. Tell me what you really want to tell me."

"He beat me up, okay?"

"I'm going to give you as much help as I can. You want to press charges? You want to file a report? You want to get away from him? I can set you up with-"

"No. I can't go to a women's shelter," she interrupts. "They're not safe." "First of all, that's not true. They are pretty safe," I say. "At least I know of a few reliable ones where people will take care of you. But there are other means as well. If you have any money at all, there are organizations that will get you an apartment in their name, help you escape. You can pay them now or later. The apartment is not going to be in your name so he won't be able to find you. It's as simple as that."

"Really?" Amelia asks.

"Yes. They are like an underground railroad, helping women."

I hand her two Excedrin after she tells me that her head hurts and I offer to take her to the hospital again.

"No. Not yet."

She takes another bite of her burger and pops a few fries in her mouth. She's famished. But she can't eat too fast because she's in excruciating pain.

"If you think that you have more to worry about, like he'll come after you, despite just moving to a different apartment, a different part of the city, then we can talk about other things," I say.

"Other things like what?"

"Well, I can help you get a new identity, a fresh start in life. Different city with witness protection. It depends on what you're trying to get away from."

"You don't have a budget for that. You're just promising things you can't deliver on."

"I've never made this promise to anyone before. I can't make guarantees. But I can tell you that I will try and I'll do my best. There is funding in the department in very special cases. But unfortunately, it's not just for people trying to get away from their abusive boyfriends."

"I mean, who cares about those women, right?" Amelia says with a tinge of sarcasm.

"It's not that. Domestic abuse is like 70% of our calls. It's the most common thing in the world. We can't relocate every single person, especially since the likelihood of her going back to him is very, very high."

"What are you getting at?" she asks, turning her torso a little bit toward me, and wincing from the pain.

"What I'm asking you is, what can you tell me about your boyfriend? What is he involved in? Who does he work for? What has he done?"

"You want to know about Kelly Flynn, don't you?"

Amelia throws three more fries into her mouth and chews slowly. Shivers run down my spine.

"Yeah. I can tell you about her. He came home that night, boasting. Said that no one will ever find out because he hid her body so well."

"Did he tell you her name?"

"No. Not then. He was drunk. I thought that he was just talking big. He's always had this big hard-on for the mafia and all the illegal gangs. He wanted to be accepted, to be part of the crew."

"What day did you have this conversation?"

"I don't remember but later that day, I saw it on the local news. They interrupted *People's Court*, my favorite show. Normally, I don't watch the news. I mean, who cares, right? But there was that bag. Some homeless man saw someone throw this bag into the LA River. It rolled and rolled. I can still remember his toothless face and all this mud and dirt on his forehead. And yet, despite all that, he looked like someone I could be friends with, you know? Someone I went to high school with. He had these piercing eyes and I remember thinking, 'Could I live like that? Under the overpass, in a tent? Having someone watch my belongings? Just drinking the days away?' Because, you know, what else is there to do but think about how crappy your life turned out?"

I give her a slight nod, commiserating.

"So, how did you know that Christian had anything to do with this body?" I ask.

"Because he was home, making hash browns in the kitchen. I called over to him and he came out. He doesn't like *People's Court*. He thought that I was showing him some case. He got annoyed. He yelled at me and told me that I need to go to law school if I'm so interested in that kind of crap."

She takes a deep breath and then continues.

"Well, I called him over and I showed him the newscast. He turned white as a ghost and I asked him if that was what he did and he said, 'Yeah.' He kind of mumbled it at first. So I asked him, 'Are you sure?' But he didn't respond. He just kept staring at the TV screen saying, 'I can't believe they found her. Nobody was supposed to be there.'"

"What happened after?" I ask quietly, partially holding my breath. She's talking now. But she could realize what she's doing. Her allegiance could change back to her boyfriend.

That's the thing about abused women. They're scared and they come forward. But, then, when they have some time to think about it, they decide that standing up to their boyfriend, or husband, would be much harder than just standing up to the police and starting a new life.

"Do you know why?" I ask.

She looks at me. Our eyes lock. Suddenly, her trance vanishes. A ping of fear tightens in my heart. What if this is it? What if she stops talking? What then?

"Is there a reason why Christian killed her?" I ask.

"He did it to impress his boss." My mouth drops open.

"Sonny?"

“No.” Amelia shakes her head. “Sonny loved her. He didn't want her to leave. They were high school sweethearts. He would've done anything for her. Well, besides stay honest. He wasn't good at fidelity but in his own way, he loved her very much. But she wanted to have full custody of their son. And he loved his son but he probably would have given it to her.”

“So, what was the problem?” I ask.

"His parents wouldn't have it."

"His mother? Is she behind this? I just knew it," I mumble to myself.

She looks at me.

"You'd think so. But, no. I mean, she's a total bitch but in this case, it was Leonard, Sonny's dad. He runs that club with an iron fist. He doesn't let anything go. And you can't really leave. You're in it for life. Even if you're an auxiliary member, like a girlfriend or a wife. Kelly knew too much. And once they were certain that she wasn't coming back, that she was filing for full custody, he put his foot down. That was it. She was gone."

"How do you know this?" I ask.

"Christian told me. He also recorded it."

"He recorded it?" My eyes grow big.

She nods.

"Leonard called Christian up one day and asked him for a favor. He refuses to text or let anyone write anything down and he talks really fast. So, when they met up, Christian was worried that he wouldn't be able to remember the address of where he was supposed to go to pick up this package. So, he got into this groove of secretly recording Leonard talking on his phone. It was just in his pocket. He pressed record and got the whole conversation. He let me listen to it. Before I left today, I took it with me."

My mouth drops open and I stare at her. Amelia takes the wrapper from the burger and wads it up into a small ball tossing it into the empty cupholder. She wipes her fingers. Then, wincing, reaches into her purse and pulls out her phone.

She finds a file. It's a recording. She just videotaped his phone. And she plays it for me.

"Listen. We need her out of here."

"Who?"

"You know who," an older voice says.

There's no video, just audio. But the quality is clear. I've never heard either of the voices before but they're both distinct, with just a little bit of background noise from cars whizzing by and the sound of the phone touching the fabric of his inside pocket.

"Who are you talking about specifically?" the younger voice asks.

"That's Christian," Amelia interrupts.

"If you do this for me as a personal favor, you're going places, kid, no matter what Sonny says," Leonard says.

"What if Sonny finds out?"

"He's not going to. You're going to do it right; you're going to follow my instructions to a T."

"This is his wife," Christian says.

"Ex-wife. And that's what makes her dangerous. She can go out there. She can date someone new. I've had her followed. She's seeing some surfer now."

"I don't know." Christian hesitates.

"You know how this game's played. Nobody leaves. You're in it for life. You put up with whatever you put up with. You think I like being married to my wife all these years? That I don't want a change? That's how it's going to be for Sonny because he made that decision. Kelly wouldn't have it that way. She didn't care that my family protected her, stood up for her, took care of that foster situation of that prick who was abusing her."

"I don't think she's going to say anything," Christian insists. But Leonard continues to push. The recording goes on for more than ten minutes. At the end, Christian reluctantly agrees.

"If you don't put me in witness protection, and if you don't protect me, they're going to kill me. I'm going to end up just like Kelly," Amelia says after I listen to the whole thing and she turns off her phone.

"Does Christian know that you have this recording?" I ask.

"Absolutely not. I don't even know if he remembers telling me about it. He's been drinking a lot and using a lot of drugs since the murder. He's never killed anyone before. He liked the leather jackets. He liked taking the oath. He just wanted to be a part of the cool kids. Maybe he just watched too much *Sons of Anarchy*."

"Can you send me this file?"

She clicks a few buttons and airdrops it to my phone. I let out a slight sigh of relief. I have something: proof. Amelia looks at me.

"I have no other choice. I can't go back there. I don't know what he'll do. He's going nuts. The guilt is eating at him. And if he's not going to kill himself, then he's going to kill me, and if Christian doesn't do it, then Leonard surely will."

I SPEND the next couple of days trying to make arrangements for Amelia without much help. I give her money out of my pocket for her to stay at a modest two-star hotel in another part of town up near Westlake in the Valley. I want to get her out of Los

Angeles and to try to protect her as best as I can, put her somewhere where no one will look for her.

The hotel is located in a nice suburban town. There's a Trader Joe's across the street and a CVS. She's never been out of LA before, and she looks around wide-eyed, surprised.

"Wow, it's all houses and condos, right?"

"Yeah. There's a park right over there."

"Homeless people? Druggies?" she asks.

I shake my head. "Not that I know of, it doesn't seem like it. There's a playground. There're kids on it now."

"That's different."

"Well, this isn't downtown LA or Hollywood. People come here to enjoy family life."

"Yeah, I wonder what that's like."

I take a seat after helping her into the hotel with a few of her belongings.

"What are you thinking about?" I ask.

She walks onto the balcony and looks out surprised, partly because there is a balcony.

I sit on the little couch next to the bed and when she returns, she says, "I think I'd like to live somewhere like this. Quiet, peaceful, a nice community, you know? I'm sick of the city and all its darkness."

"Well, we can try to get that done. It's going to be a little bit before I can get you into the LA Witness Protection Program. I've never gone through the process before and it is quite difficult, but you're an important witness and I'll do my best."

"What if it doesn't work out?"

"I'm going to pay for this room and I want you to move around. I'll book you a few others. Right now I want you to change hotels every afternoon. I don't want you talking to anyone, and if you do, you tell each person a different story."

"Like what?"

"You tell them that you're from Pennsylvania. You're here visiting your aunt. Don't talk to any men just in case. Wear frumpy clothes."

"Yeah, well, given how I look now, I don't really want anyone to see me at all."

"Good, keep it that way," I say, nervously cracking my knuckles.

29

Days go by and I continue to work trying to get Amelia into the witness protection program. I talk to Captain Medvil and Catherine multiple times, not to much avail, the cases are backed up. Additional paperwork needs to be filed. When I try to reach the higher ups, they say, they're busy. Meanwhile, the search continues for Christian Bertrand.

With the recording and the DNA evidence that we found on Kelly's body it was enough to open an investigation and get a search warrant. He is the primary suspect. We kept the recording and everything else that we have on him secret from the media, but that didn't stop things from leaking and getting out. There was speculation on YouTube and blogs about how Christian was involved. People are speculating that they had met in a bar and they'd had a previous relationship.

These are all amateur investigators and they don't have his history on hand. No access to previous aliases. He had never officially testified against the Nighthawks in any capacity and there are only a few photos of him in the cut, a cutoff jacket with the club's patches. So far, just a few online investigators have made his connection to the Nighthawks.

The more days that pass, the more scared Amelia gets. When I ask if I should call her by her real name, Sarah, she insists on Amelia. I guess naming herself gives her a sense of power. She grew up in a cult and she wants to get as far away from her given name as possible. Finally, Catherine reaches out with good news: Amelia's witness status is going to be approved. She also tells me that I would be reimbursed for all of the rooms that I had paid for.

We also get word that an off-duty officer had spotted someone who looks a lot like Christian in a bar in San Ysidro, a town near the Mexican border.

He had just gotten a briefing earlier in the day and even though the picture that he'd snapped of this man sitting next to him had professionally lightened hair and a considerable tan, as well as a button-down shirt with a suit jacket, I could see the resemblance right away.

I've never seen him wear a suit in my life. Amelia texted after getting the picture. *But it's definitely him.*

I get in touch with someone at the station. Once I confirm that it was definitely him, his parole officer gave us the go ahead to arrest him and sent the local police for backup.

I get into my car and start driving toward the precinct, calling Amelia on the way.

"He doesn't look anything like himself," she mumbles.

"That's kind of the point," I say, slowing down for a red light and sitting in bumper-to-bumper traffic on Melrose. "The suit was a good move, to tell you the truth."

We were on the lookout for someone who looks like a criminal, casual clothes, maybe a leather jacket or a hoodie. Nobody is looking for a real estate agent.

"He cut his hair, too," she says. "Quite short, professional looking. He looks like an accountant."

I nod.

"He knows what he is doing," I admit. "It's a good thing that guy found him because if he had gotten into Mexico…"

My voice trails off.

"He would have vanished," Amelia finishes my thought.

When I get to the precinct, I wait for news with a small group of people who are familiar with the case.

Catherine is there and we listen to the frequencies, trying to hear of any news.

"How's Amelia?" Catherine asks, shifting her weight nervously from foot to foot. "You think it's him? Did you see his face?"

The questions come at me, rapid fire. Like they're being shot out of a gun. I don't even get a chance to answer one before the next one approaches.

"Sorry, I'm just really nervous," she admits. "I really hope that we can take him and nothing happens."

"It's going to be fine," I insist.

Truthfully, I don't know that any more than she does. It's all out of my hands.

The off-duty officer spotted him in the bar and snapped a photo. He's a rookie, first year on the job. Generally, cops just take someone in, but he wanted to make sure that it was really Christian. It's a big deal to point a gun into an innocent person's face if it's not the right guy.

The rookie didn't want that on this record, so he was being cautious. I get it. But still I wish that he had at least put him in handcuffs and then sent for confirmation.

Captain Medvil comes out of his office, his eyes wide, face flushed and flustered.

“He's on the run! They didn't get him!” he says, sipping wildly on the big 72 ounce cup of soda, which would come sloshing out if it didn’t have a thick lid.

We flip on the news. A police helicopter provides the video footage.

"What happened?" I ask.

"That idiot cop should have arrested him first,” Captain Medvil steams. "As soon as he called them, the guy took off and the backup wasn't there yet. He got out through the back. Apparently, the rookie barely passed the running exam."

“That’s why the physical is important, ladies and gentlemen,” Captain Medvil says sarcastically. “You're not always in a fricking car. I keep telling that to the higher ups and they just don't get it.”

30

I spend the rest of the day watching the story unfold. At the precinct, I'm tempted to get into a car, patrol or otherwise, but it's at least a three hour drive. And with the traffic it'll probably be more.

This isn't just going to San Diego, mind you, this is going all the way to the border. But Medvil says no; he needs me here for when they bring in the rest of the suspects.

I find myself on pins and needles. I keep going back to the vending machine for more and more snacks that I should not be eating. Junk food is something I always crave in times of crisis and boredom. That's what contributed to me gaining all of this extra weight the last year.

I started out pretty thin and now I'm hovering on overweight, and at this rate, it's going to get worse. As I wait, going back and forth from my desk to the main area, to the vending machine, walking past Catherine's office and back again, I keep picking at my nails, biting a few of them down all the way to the nubs.

Catherine is hiding out in her office.

"You don't want to be out there?" I ask.

"Just needed some quiet time."

I continue to chew on the ring finger of my left hand. She gives me a look and then kicks out the chair in front of her desk. I catch it as it starts to fall.

"I just wish that I could be there, you know?"

"What would you do?"

"Well, sometimes just driving around in the patrol car makes me feel like I'm doing something, being productive."

"Well, they're bringing in the rest. Sonny, Leonard, Dolores, the whole gang."

"What about Amelia?" I ask.

"As long as she's still in that hotel room, then we're good. If she flees, then we don't have much of a case."

Despite the long day, Catherine's eyeliner is still perfect. The rest of her makeup is also flawless. Her hair is shiny as if she has just come out of the salon. She doesn't look the least bit phased, but when she presses her lips to the Starbucks latte, I can see the facade crack just a little bit.

"How do you look like that?" I blurt out. "Just so unfazed, not even tired."

"Years of practice. You kind of have to put on this mask. Makeup helps."

"What about your hair? I mean, look at mine, a few hours in and the heat and the air conditioning gets to it and it just looks worn out. Not exactly one of those hot television cops they always have parading around in their heels and their black suits screaming professionalism."

"Screaming professionalism, is that what they're doing?" Catherine smiles, sitting back in her chair and unbuttoning her jacket. "I've always liked to wear this kind of stuff. If you can imagine, when I was in high school I dressed up a lot."

"You were president of your class, weren't you?"

"Of course."

I laugh, tilting my head.

"Want some coffee?"

I nod, starting to get up, but she lifts up her manicured index finger and points to the espresso machine next to her.

"I paid a lot of money for this and it should probably be a write-off but the department's refusing to approve it."

"I bet if you take that job at that private law firm, you can get something like that and you wouldn't even have to pay for it."

"Yeah, probably, but then I wouldn't get to take down bad guys." Catherine winks.

"Do you think you'll take it?"

"Not sure, still considering it."

"What's stopping you?"

"Cases like this. I just keep thinking about what happened to Kelly Flynn and how much I want to make those bastards pay for killing her."

"Being a prosecutor has some perks," I point out.

"I hate to say it, but it just gets me going, you know, in the morning? I can pretend all I want that there's a reason why people do bad things. I know that there is psychology, their history, their terrible parents, but at the end of the day, I feel like some people are just pricks, bad guys and I love being in the position to make them pay for what they have done."

"Is that what you're going to do to Christian?" I ask.

"Yeah, I hope so, if they give me a chance."

"May I?"

There's a small television in the corner and she gives me a slight nod of approval.

"Sure. Go ahead," she says. "Turn it on. Might as well hear the latest update."

But as soon as the local news comes on, my face falls. I glance over to her to make sure that what I'm hearing is right. She has the same grave expression on her face as I do.

"A few minutes ago, the body of Christian Bertrand, the man suspected of killing Kelly Flynn," the newscaster says, "was found. He shot himself in the head after being cornered by an off-duty police officer who spotted him in a border town bar. He was planning on crossing the border tomorrow morning during rush hour and disappearing into Mexico. That's all the information we have at this point, but stay tuned because we'll have an official report from the authorities shortly."

I stare at the screen as it goes into a commercial and photographs of Kelly and Christian fade from view.

"He killed himself?" Catherine whispers.

"I guess so," I say, shaking my head in disbelief.

The news woman was standing in front of police tape and in the background, I see cops peeking over into the car he had been driving. The license plate is not obscured and is identical to the one I had memorized. My phone rings and I answer knowing that it's Amelia.

"He's dead? Are you sure he's dead?" she asks, her voice going up at the end of each question.

"Yes, I'm sorry."

"Don't be. I'm so relieved," she says, taking me by surprise. "I'm glad that he's gone. He's not going to hurt me anymore."

She lets out a sigh of relief.

"I wasn't sure if I'd be able to testify against him. I wasn't sure if you'd be able to keep me safe. But now ..."

"Amelia," I say quietly, "I still need your help. He wasn't the only one involved in this."

"No, I can't," she whispers.

"I'm going to come right over and we're going to have a chat. Okay?"

She hesitates but I press. Eventually, she agrees.

"Let me get a drink?" I ask, looking at Catherine.

"Aren't you going over to talk to your witness?"

"Yeah, but not right this minute. I need a break. It's been a long day."

We get to the bar for happy hour. It's packed with cops and a few unsuspecting civilians. I order a vodka on the rocks and she opts for a cosmopolitan. We nurse our drinks for as long as possible, not wanting to get another round because we're both planning on working late into the night.

"What now?" I ask, tapping my fingers on the table, speaking a little too loudly for comfort, but being unable to do anything about it since everyone else is practically shouting.

"Not sure." She furrows her brows and tilts her head to one side. "Didn't exactly get to put the bad guy away."

"There's Leonard," I say, raising an eyebrow.

She looks like she's having some doubts about being able to build a good case.

"Well, Christian did kill himself. That's evidence of *something*," I continue. "We have his recording and we have Amelia who's terrified and scared to death, not just of her ex-boyfriend, but now the Nighthawks in general."

"Yeah, but you just need to make some magic happen," she says, and I raise one eyebrow as I take a sip of my drink.

The ice has all but melted leaving me with the glare of an annoyed bartender waiting for us to clear these seats in lieu of better customers.

"I don't know if we're going to have much of a case but we have to try, right? I mean, you know what that guy did and we have a recording of it."

"Can it be admitted into court?" I ask.

"This is going to be hard. The fact that Amelia has seen it and listened to it herself is going to go a long way in making it happen, but it's going to depend largely on the type of judge we get and the case that I build."

"But, if you're leaving to take that other job…"

"No, I'm not going to go yet. Seems to me that the other job is going to be around for a while and I still have some good work to do around here."

I chuckle.

"You're a lifer," I say. "You're one of those DAs who dreams of going and doing something else, but the most exciting part of it all for you is just to imagine what it would be like. It's like I watch all these videos on YouTube about living in a cabin in the mountains and the snow, but do I really want to do that? I mean, *really*?"

"That sounds like heaven," Catherine says.

"Tell you the truth, I'm not sure that's really what I want. I mean, I grew up in a town like that and there's this nostalgia associated with it. And so it keeps bringing me back and the algorithm keeps recommending more and more single women staking their claim in all of these cabins that they renovate and then live this bucolic hobbit-kind of life in them. But if I were pressed on the issue, I'm not sure it's for me, at least not for many, many years."

She tilts her head. "I kind of think you're right. Maybe I am a lifer."

"Hey, at least we can be here serving the population being severely underpaid and under-appreciated *together*, forever."

"I like that."

I nod, extending my hand and then pulling her in for a quick hug.

"Okay. I have to go talk to our witness. I hope she doesn't take off on me and ruin this case once and for all."

"Go get her.” Catherine laughs and I walk away.

31

A bit later, I return to Big Bear after taking a few well deserved days off. I should probably stay home and relax, but I haven't seen my mom for a while and I want to check to see if there has been any progress on the case and talk to a few more people.

Sometimes, at times like this, it's better to re-interview everyone again. Luke returns with me.

I haven't seen him for a while and I miss being in his arms. I visit Mom, but opt to get a room at the Robin Hood Inn just to have some quiet time with Luke. As soon as he comes in and sees my stuff spread all over the room, he starts to complain, jokingly, of course, but I know that in comparison to how neat he is, I can't exactly compete.

We talk about the case and what happened with Christian, and I ask him about Kansas. He doesn't share too much, a little bit here and there.

He tells me that his mom sends her love. I don't get the sense that he's hiding something, just that our two work schedules are making it difficult to maintain any semblance of what a relationship should be.

"All we talk about is work," he says. "Let's change that."

"I agree."

We order a pizza and I eat way too much. While chewing on the last bit of the crust, I tell him that I'm planning to interview more of the same witnesses.

"You mean here, in Violet's case?" he asks.

"Yeah, of course. What else can I do? It's been a while. Maybe their stories have changed. Maybe there's some detail that they didn't mention. Who knows?”

He nods.

"I wish that I could help. I know that this is difficult for you.”

"Oh, sorry!” Smacking my forehead, I realize that I had just promised him that we'd talk about something besides work. "It's just the only thing that's on my mind. It, like, consumes me, you know?"

"Yeah, I know." He nods. "That's why this work is so difficult. You can't unplug. You can't do anything else."

When I stop by my mom's house, we don't discuss anything with much substance. I'm tempted to bring up Violet but it seems to be all that we talk about. I know I need to find Captain Talarico to get an update, but I'm afraid that he'll tell me that I shouldn't be interviewing the witnesses again, since I'm not officially on the case.

So, I opt to do it on my own.

Of course, I want to talk to Neil the most, but after what happened before, I stay away. Instead, I head to the pizza shop and much to my surprise, I run into Natalie's brothers.

It's been a few hours since I ate and I'm still ridiculously full. But I buy a salad to have a reason to stay without being suspicious. I sit in the booth to the side of them and listen in.

"Aren't you Violet's sister?" one says.

"Uh-huh," I mumble. And then clear my throat and repeat it. "Yes, I am."

"You here to talk to us?"

"I didn't know you would be here, but yeah, I am here to have a little chat." I admit. "Just want to ask you some more questions."

"You don't have any answers for us?" Michael says. "I mean, you're the big time LAPD detective, right? You have nothing on this sheriff's station in a small town. You should have the answers."

"I wish we had some. I've been working closely with them, but I don't know what could have happened. They're still running tests."

"That's what they say all the time. Just more and more tests. What they don't want to admit publicly is that they have absolutely nothing and no clues to go on *whatsoever*. Maybe they contaminated the crime scene. What do you think about that?"

I've heard rumors of that. I don't dare to admit it, but I tell him that those have been the whispers on a number of sites that I've been tracking.

“Like where?” Steven asks.

“Nextdoor, Facebook, Instagram, TikTok, and some message board strings as well that are devoted solely to this case online.”

"Is there anything that you can tell me besides what you told the police? Anything additional?"

"I don't know what you want from me," Steven says, giving out a big sigh. "I mean, we already gave like a million statements and no one can find a thing. I have no idea what she did. I don't even know what's relevant and what's not relevant."

"What about anything about your friendship with Neil? Anything that you did beforehand or after? Anything unusual? Any unusual place you've been?"

"Well, we usually just hung out at his house or our house. A few times we played basketball at the park. Went skiing. I've never been to that cabin of his though, but I'm not sure why that would be of interest."

"Cabin?" I go through my mental notes trying to remember if anyone had ever mentioned a cabin. "What kind of cabin?"

"Not really a cabin. I have no idea," Steven says, shaking his head, taking a bite of his pizza.

"His family has a cabin somewhere in the mountains?" I ask.

"No, out in the desert. He mentioned it once. It's like a hunting cabin. His dad's a big hunter. There are antelope there."

"And you've never been there?" I ask.

"Nope."

"How about you, Michael?" I ask.

He shakes his head no. "Does that matter? Do you think it has some significance?"

"I don't know, and you said you mentioned this to the police?"

"Yeah. Maybe. I'm not sure actually." They look at each other, the way that twins do, finishing each other's sentences.

I open my notebook with all the notes I've taken on the case, interviews and everything else. There's no mention of a cabin.

"Do you happen to know where it is besides the desert?" I ask.

"I'm pretty sure it's in some place called Pioneertown."

"Is that even a real place?" the other one asks.

"Yes, it is." I nod. "It's right near Yucca Valley."

"Kind of like near Joshua Tree?" Michael asks.

"Yeah, that's right. It's like an old west town."

"I think I heard something about it," Steven says.

32

After the boys leave, I stay behind for a while, thinking about what they have just said. The Goss family has a cabin in the desert, a cabin that no one has mentioned before.

What could this mean? Probably nothing.

Or... No.

It doesn't make sense.

What I can't quite get my head around is that if Neil had something to do with this and the cabin is somehow involved, what about Natalie's body?

I head back home, my mind still going in circles about all the possibilities.

At the hotel room that I'm sharing with Luke, I find him in front of the television, mindlessly watching an old episode of *Law and Order: SVU*.

I tell him about the cabin but, much to my surprise, his eyes don't light up. "Don't you see what this means?" I insist. "This could be big."

"Or, it could be nothing."

"I know, but..."

"I just don't want you to get your hopes up," Luke says.

He sits up against the headboard and takes a big gulp of his coffee. He's always been the type to drink it late at night somehow without it affecting him one bit. We've talked about it a number of times.

I still don't understand why he would drink it in the morning if he's not getting the caffeine kick? But I've yet to hear a good explanation.

He takes another big gulp.

"Look, what do you want me to say?" he asks.

"I want you to be excited. This could be a huge break in the case."

"Yeah, or it could be nothing."

"But, they kind of hid this fact from us, right?"

"Apparently not. Not if the brothers knew. I mean... Look, I'm not trying to rain on your parade," Luke says, walking over to me and taking me into his arms. "But I want you to take care of yourself. You just get so worked up."

"This is a big deal. You know that. You're an FBI agent."

"I know. But if everyone knew about the cabin, they would have probably investigated it."

"I'm going to call Talarico right now."

I pick up my phone, but he pulls it out of my hand.

"You can't. It's ten o'clock at night. You're going to wake him up and ask him about *this*?"

"I don't think he's sleeping yet."

"Okay. His wife."

"I have to do something," I say.

"Let's just think about it. Let's just wait. If they thought that you already knew, then they probably told the cops and it's probably a known thing. So, what's another few hours going to do?"

I shrug. Sitting down on the edge of the bed, I can't help but want to agree with him. It is late at night. The drive is long and I don't exactly have an address.

"Come here," Luke says, pulling me closer and tugging on my shirt. But I'm not in the mood. I give him a little chaste kiss and pull away.

"I'm really tired. It's been an awfully long day."

"Okay." He admits defeat.

I go into the bathroom and brush my teeth, wash my face, and climb under the covers. Luke sits on the bed next to me, then strips off his shirt and lies back down.

Turning off the light, nothing but the blue from the TV screen illuminates our faces. Detective Benson runs fast and yells a lot and I remember how much the show influenced me in my desire to become a detective. However, action-packed, this job is not.

There are probably a few hours of action crammed into a year's worth of work and the rest of it is a lot of talking, asking questions, and piles of paperwork.

I close my eyes, listening to the hum of the television and hoping it will drag me off to sleep, but I don't have much luck. One episode turns into two, and then into three.

Luke has already started to snore. He has turned away from me with his head tucked into the crook of his elbow. He means well, but he isn't always right. There're just certain things that you have to do in life, even if you don't want to, so you can get the right answers.

I sneak out of bed and open my laptop away from the bed, so that the blue light doesn't wake up Luke. I search the Goss family name first, comparing the exact spelling of everyone's name with the names on my notepad. Then, I enter Neil's father's name into the real estate search, finding nothing but the main house. I try his mother's name, but again, it just lists their main house.

Could the boys have been wrong?

Perhaps, but it's likely that there is a cabin. Maybe it's just not located in Pioneertown. Maybe it's in Yucca Valley or Joshua Tree, or somewhere else in that area.

What was the name of that other town? I wonder to myself.

Oh, yeah. Landers!

It's an even smaller unincorporated community in the flatlands of the desert above, slightly above the Yucca Valley hills.

Maybe there's something that I missed. The house was registered in a family member's name, but whom?

How would I ever find them?

The main family listing comes up with the names of few people who may or may not be associated with the family.

James Gaugren.

Emily Claire.

Ann Broader.

Eric Thomas Giffin.

I search each one but the first three don't seem to have any connection.

When I try the last one, whose age is listed about twenty-five years older than Neil's father, I get the address of a place in Pioneertown.

This must be it, I say to myself.

I mean, it could be someone's random house, but what are the chances? I do one last search for Eric Thomas Giffin.

Facebook, of all places, and see that the connection to his son, is none other than Mr. Goss.

It's him, I say to myself. It's actually him.

After closing the laptop as quietly as possible, I start to pack. I change out of my clothes and into a pair of jeans, a loose-fitting top, and a hoodie. I have a long drive ahead of me.

I don't have a warrant and I don't have much of a plan of what I'm going to do, but I have to inspect the property and make sure that there's nothing there that I have missed.

I hold my breath as I exit the hotel room, making sure that I'm not making too much noise. I don't want to wake Luke up.

I don't want to have an argument. After all, Luke is likely right.

I have no plan. But I have to do this. I have no other choice.

I DRIVE the back way to Yucca Valley on 18 and then 247 through Lucerne and Johnson Valley. The roads are deserted and it's dark, no streetlights. It's down an enormous mountain into the flat empty valley below. I've always loved the desert, the wide-open spaces, the bright blue sky. It's a complete contrast to the mountain town where I grew up and even more of a contrast to the hustle and bustle of the city and the ocean and the waves that it's surrounded by. I drive alone, which is probably better than if I were to have one set of headlights behind me or ahead of me.

I don't know where I'm going. I have an address, but I don't know what awaits me. It's about a two-hour drive.

At first, it's down a winding mountain road and then it levels off and it's straight for miles and miles. I made sure that I had enough gas at the top of the hill, and now I just cruise, anxiously awaiting whatever lies ahead.

What can I expect? I don't know.

My heart closes up when I think about possibly seeing Violet again but the detective in me says that I'm going there to look for *remains*. If there's anything to find at all.

The cabin could just be another false lead like everything else has been. It's an all-too-common existence for a situation like this, especially when the perpetrator is smart and cunning and isn't caught in the first forty-eight hours.

They say that, "It's darkest before dawn" and there's truth in that. When I head over the mountains and into Yucca Valley, I see the lights of the town of about 25,000 people. It's just waking up as the sun is spreading its rays over the valley. I've been here a few times on my way to Joshua Tree National Park, a beautiful gem of a place with enormous boulders and crooked trees unlike those that grow in any other part of the world.

At night, and in these early moments of dawn, they look like something out of a Tim Burton movie. Jagged edges, menacing, and frightful. The trees don't want the birds to pick them clean. They don't want the animals of the desert to eat their core. The spikes are their way to protect themselves and to survive in this harsh environment where water is so limited, but beauty is in so much balance and is so abundant.

When I get to Yucca Valley and drive through the beautiful boulder-lined Western Estates area I pull into the gas station and check out the address on Google Maps. The house is less than twenty minutes away, and the anxiety of what I'm about to find there is getting bad.

I force myself out of the car and into the little shop. I browse the aisles for candy and junk food before making myself a cup of hot tea, Earl Grey, and getting a pack of nachos with fresh hot cheese.

That thing about eating junk food when I'm particularly nervous and feeling out of control is exactly what's going on here. It's not normally anything I'd have this early in the morning and I try to avoid it entirely, but the cravings are sky high and I haven't had any sleep tonight, making the nachos impossible to resist.

It's going to be okay, I say to myself silently over and over again, trying to make myself believe with that positive attitude that we all hear about. Somehow it doesn't exactly click.

When I get back to the car, I sit at the steering wheel and eat my nachos, taking my time and lingering on each bite.

I'm killing time. It's not right. I should just head right on over but the decision to do this has been taken a little too lightly and suddenly it's all dawning on me.

I'm here by myself.

What I'm looking for I don't know. And if I get the right answers, the Goss family is not going to be happy. Yet, I did not call for backup. I did not tell anyone back home or at the sheriff's department here what I'm doing. I have no warrant.

Unless somebody lets me in, I have no right to be there. I should have at least brought Luke, but he made it clear that he would stop me from coming.

Asking forgiveness is easier than asking permission. Yet working on the last nacho chip and dipping it in the last bit of the cheese at five o'clock in the morning, I regret the fact that I don't have anyone with me.

I do have a weapon and it's something, but no warrant, which would be preferred. As a police officer we've all been drilled to believe that we need a warrant to do anything. There are certain circumstances in which you can, of course, force a car door open, arrest someone, or do any number of other things in your line of duty.

But in this case, no one's life is in danger and if I were to find remains, a shiver runs down my spine, along with a bit of cold sweat, it would be a difficult thing to get admitted into court.

Still, I'm here. I have to find out.

I take a deep breath, run my finger along the last bit of the cheese, and start the engine.

33

The GPS takes me back into the wild hills away from the town. I look at my cell reception, no bars left. I've been to Pioneertown before. It's a little Western place that used to be a set for 1950's TV shows. The buildings are still up and there are a few businesses operating ad hoc, selling fabrics and soap made out of goat's milk. But it's all very under the surface, no licensing and not even any electricity.

I drive past Pappy and Harriet's, a saloon bar where big-name acts like The White Buffalo and The White Stripes like to perform secret shows. It's one of those under the radar LA joints for only those in the know, and for those who can get tickets.

Pappy and Harriet's is closed.

With the dawn just breaking, I head past the wall of green cacti illuminated by the pastel colors and I say to myself that it's finally getting bright enough that I'm not going to be stumbling around in the dark. There are enormous boulders lining each side of the narrow canyon and I see my turnoff, a dirt road, is coming up.

I drive for close to four miles and it takes a good half an hour. My tires pick up rocks and toss them aside, and I drive slowly knowing that from the hills all around, anyone can spot me coming from miles ahead. Suddenly, I regret my bright blue 2015 Prius, a pretty memorable and recognizable vehicle. I wish that I had opted for a truck or something else instead, but definitely not a patrol car.

Out in the distance, I see a small cabin nestled into the hills. I know from my research that this house has a ten acre plot of land attached to it and no neighbors nearby. I looked at it on Google to familiarize myself. The latest listing also shows the house inside from when they tried to sell it four years ago.

It's a three-bedroom with one-bathroom. It's not new, but it looks like it has been remodeled. I drive a little bit down the road just past it, slowing down even more to take my time. There is a sandy driveway covered with gravel leading up to the house and no cars anywhere around it.

"No one is home," I say. "Good."

I decide to park on the road about half a mile away from the house itself. The place is nestled in the hills and I look out in the distance but see no one. The hills are dark as the sun is coming up, just barely illuminating them and washing them in hues of pink and peach.

There's a gate and a fence around the property and I leave my car to the side of it. It's not very tall so I easily hop it. I head toward the hills, following the trail and the other part of the fence. If someone were to spot me, they might think I'm a hiker, allowing me to get closer to the house without trespassing. Not quite yet.

I approach the house carefully. It's one story with a fresh coat of paint all around and a bright white wooden door.

Honestly, it looks like a place that has recently been remodeled for a Joshua Tree desert style Airbnb. There's even a hot tub to one side and a beautiful deck with Adirondack chairs facing the mountains.

I hesitate for a moment trying to decide what to do.

Do I just break in? Do I wait? There are no cars here.

I could hop the fence, try to check out the house, and try to find something, anything, but what?

When the sun comes over the mountains, something falls inside the house. A loud yelp belonging to a woman startles me.

I grab onto the fence and jump, running over to the window and peeking inside.

"Violet?" I yell.

I run around to the front. The door is locked. I pound on it with my fists. Someone scrambles inside.

Peeking into the window, I see her hovering by the dining room table. She sits on the floor with her knees to her chin shaking.

"Violet, I'm coming!" I yell.

But she just shakes her head and raises her hand slightly in my direction. I reach for my nine millimeter handgun that I have tucked in the back of my jeans. I brought it just in case, backup. It's an FN509MRD-LE.

It's only available to law enforcement agencies and something that was just issued to me at the department. It feels heavy in my hand, but I steady it as I make my way around the house, keeping my back to the wall.

"I'm coming, Violet!" I yell, trying the door by keeping my profile from standing directly in front of it.

This door's locked, too, but it's a small glitchy kind of lock that looks like it's easy to open. I take a few steps away and kick at the lock and the frame.

Violet begins to whimper.

I rush over to her and find her right hand handcuffed to the radiator next to the dining room table. She can stand up, but she can't make it too far away.

"You're going to be okay. You're going to be okay. I'm here," I whisper, holding her.

She seems to recognize me, but only slightly. She's groggy, sedated, clearly drugged.

"What are you doing here?" I ask her over and over again, not expecting any answers.

I try the lock. I look around for the key. The dining room is small and connected to the kitchen and the living room. The ceilings are low. This is an old 1950's cabin that was added onto over the years.

"Is anyone here?" I ask, even though I have already made my way around the three small bedrooms and the bathroom to make sure it's empty.

"Is anyone coming back?"

She shakes her head no, and then shrugs.

Her responses are delayed. It's like she's here, but not.

She's dressed in clothes I've never seen. Black leggings, white socks, flannel shirt that's way too big and looks like it belongs to a man. Her hair hasn't been washed in weeks and she has sores on her face. She's lost maybe a little bit of weight, but not that much. So, at least someone has been feeding her.

"We have to get out of here," I tell her and a few seconds later, she nods. "Do you know if there's a key to this anywhere?" I look straight into her eyes and try to focus them.

"Please, you have to help. Is there a key somewhere?"

"I don't know," she says very, very slowly.

Each word comes out with great effort.

"The fridge," she whispers when I bump around the drawers in the kitchen, but find nothing.

I open the fridge, look inside, look in the freezer and all around.

"What are you talking about?" I ask, but she just lets out a deep sigh of relief, almost like she's giving up.

I continue to look. I keep an eye out for some pins just in case I spot anything and I'll try to pick the lock, but I'm not too good at that.

Just as I'm about to give up, I grab onto something small and metal, rounded on one edge and jagged on the other, and when I pull it down, I see that it's a small key.

It's the kind that would fit into a pair of handcuffs.

"I got it." I rush over to Violet, but she barely responds.

My hand trembles but when I put the key in the lock and turn it the handcuffs pop open.

"I got it, I got it!" I yell, pulling Violet up to her feet, but she just stares at me dumbfounded with a vacant expression in her eyes.

It's like she's high on opioids, something that she has never done before. The bastard drugged her, I say to myself.

"Come on, we have to get out of here," I say, pulling at her, but she can't really walk.

Her legs are folding under her. I prop her up with my shoulder, wrapping her arms around me.

"Please. Please, help me."

She's gotten bigger, taller somehow, or maybe it's just been a while since I held her in my arms. A human body that doesn't cooperate is incredibly difficult to carry. Someone can be 110 pounds but if the body is limp, it becomes quite difficult because of the weight distribution. I'm lucky in that Violet is breathing, alive, and here. Not exactly fully present, but I'll deal with that later.

"You're fine. You're going to be fine," I say with tears starting to stream down my face.

I help her to the front door and open the lock. When I walk out onto the porch, a burst of cool air washes over me and I suddenly feel a wave of relief.

This whole time a part of me had assumed that I was coming here looking for her dead body. All of the searches that we organized, people were looking for evidence, parts, pieces of clothing.

I can't possibly describe what it's like to go to search after search looking for body parts and now finding her alive.

I let out a big sigh of relief.

“I’m going to get you out of here," I say.

When she turns her face toward me and I wipe off some of the caked-on dirt, I see a tear run down the outside of her cheek, making a little trail through the grime.

"It's okay, don't cry. It's going to be fine."

With her arm draped over my shoulder and mine firmly around her waist, I manage to make it nearly all the way to the front of the gate before the first shot hits the ground.

It's just a little bit in front of me.

The sound ricochets, stunning me for a moment and I immediately look for cover.

I'm tempted to run over to the gate and to keep going, but my car is parked all the way at the far end of the fence and I'm sure we won't be able to make it. Once I realize from which direction the shots are coming from, I pull Violet to the big boulder to one side and hide behind it.

Somebody is using a sniper rifle. I see him out in the distance, but he's not reaching us, we are just out of range.

"Crap," I say, with my heart pounding out of my chest.

I grab my phone out of my back pocket and call for backup, identifying myself as an LAPD officer.

"I rescued my sister," I say, stumbling over my words. "Violet Carr, she has been missing from Big Bear Lake for quite some time. I found her in this cabin."

I rattle off the address in Pioneertown.

"Please come as soon as you can. Someone is shooting at us with a sniper rifle. I'm hiding out behind a boulder but I don't know how much time I have."

The 911 operator keeps me on the line and I say a few silent prayers as she continues to ask me questions. It is police policy keep the caller talking until help gets there.

But I need time to figure out what to do. I can't talk to her right now, not while our lives are in danger.

"The officers need to come, but I can't stay on the line," I say after a long pause. "I need to protect myself and my sister. You have to understand."

"Okay, but at least put the phone down and keep me on," she instructs. "I want to know what's going on."

I slip the phone into my front pocket and keep it on, hoping that it doesn't record our deaths.

34

I cover Violet's head as the shots keep coming and I try to figure out what to do.

I pull out my handgun. It's incredibly reliable with unmatched accuracy from a striker-fired handgun. It was tested beyond one million rounds and chosen by the department for its compatibility with a wide variety of training and duty ammunition. It's a 9mm, double action with a mag capacity of seventeen rounds.

Not too few, but not too many either.

I can't just shoot at the mountain in blind hope of trying to get someone. The guy with the rifle has a scope. He's hitting way too close for comfort.

"Who is that?" I ask Violet. "Who is shooting at us?"

But she just stares at me in vain. It has to be someone in the Goss family, but Neil? Is this really Neil doing this?

I hear a burst of fire near me and I shoot in that direction. I resist the urge to empty the magazine, knowing that I need to save my ammunition.

A few little rocks fall down to the ground. It's the sound of running feet.

I grab onto Violet as I get the sense that *he's* coming closer. I have one choice to make, left or right, around the boulder.

It's a blind choice.

I can't tell which way the guy's coming from.

When I hear a few more footsteps, I run left, pulling Violet with me.

"Drop the gun," someone says.

I've made the wrong choice. My heart sinks.

The voice is a low baritone. I can't quite place it until I look up.

It belongs to Timothy Goss, Neil's father.

He points the rifle at Violet and tells me to drop the gun again. When I hesitate, he shoots at her feet. Much to my surprise, she doesn't make a move to jump out of the way. The sound echoes all around the canyon.

"You better listen to me, otherwise you're both going to end up dead right now."

I lower my arm and drop the gun to the ground. Goss reaches his foot over and kicks it.

My heart pounds and sloshes so loudly in my head that I can barely hear a word that anyone is saying, let alone my thoughts.

"What are you doing here?" I ask.

"That's a better question for you, isn't it? How'd you find me?"

"Why is Violet here? Why are you keeping her here, Mr. Goss?" I ask, still using the formal title out of habit.

"That's a difficult question to answer."

"Please, I have to know."

"Well, since you're a dead woman walking, I guess you deserve some answers. You have done a lot of research and work, and I, of all people, know how hard it is to *not* know something."

"Did you *kill* Natalie?" I ask when he hesitates for a moment, clearing his throat.

He's dressed in khaki pants and a work shirt, no suit or jacket like before. His face is covered in a thin layer of dust.

"What were you doing out there?" I ask.

If he's not willing to answer questions about Natalie or Violet, maybe he'll tell me something else.

"I was hunting. Spent the night here. This is my place to get away from work and family and decompress."

"And Violet and Natalie?" I ask.

I wait for him to say that he had nothing to do with Natalie's death, but he doesn't.

"Did Neil do this?" I ask.

He shakes his head no.

"Neil doesn't know anything about this. The girls came around the house. He was dating them, friendly with them, and they're really pretty. They kind of reminded me of my wife back when we met, so I figured what if one of them just disappeared? How would anyone know that I was involved?"

“So, you *took* Violet?" I ask in a gasp.

"Yeah. But don't worry. I didn't traumatize her."

"Not at all?" I tilt my head, pretending like I actually believe him.

I lean my body against the boulder and when he looks away from me, I search for something hard to grab.

Violet continues to sit in a half-comatose state, here but not here, straddling two worlds at once.

"*Why* is she like this?" I ask.

"She was very upset. I needed to calm her down. But every time it wore off, she got angry again."

“So, you just kept drugging her?" I ask.

"I thought that one of these days, she'd cooperate. But I wanted to keep her alive. I'm not a sadistic person, Ms. Carr. I didn't want to hurt her, but she didn't understand. Every time she came to, she'd start yelling and trying to attack me. She wasn't very cooperative."

Good girl, I say silently to myself. "What about Natalie?" I ask.

"Well, Violet didn't work out, so I figured maybe Natalie would."

"You wanted to just take them here and do what?"

"Be with me. Have fun. Live here. I'll take care of them. I just wanted them to know that I cared about them."

"But everyone was looking for them."

"Yeah, but they'd never look in the District Attorney's home, especially *not* one registered to him. Very few people know about this place. I told my wife that we sold it a while ago, but her father and I were very close. We understood each other. He said that it's good to have a place where you can be a man, where you can do what you want to do, away from your family."

I feel sick to my stomach.

How am I ever going to get out of here?

How am I ever going to save Violet's life?

I tell myself to stay calm. Freaking out is only going to make this worse. "But why was Natalie's body found back in Big Bear?" I ask. "They didn't find any evidence on her either."

"No, they didn't. I did a good job of that. One day, she had an allergic reaction to something because I was keeping the girls separate, you know, so they wouldn't try to coordinate their efforts. Not sure how. Found her dead."

"Allergic reaction to what?" I ask.

"Fentanyl and meth. I've had this drug combination going that seemed to work well until it didn't."

"Not really an allergic reaction then, huh? More like a drug overdose."

He shrugs and flashes a smile.

I shake my head. I'm tempted to argue, or better yet, punch him in his gut, but he still has the rifle pointed straight at me and I'm my sister's only help.

“But how did you do this?” I ask. “Take them?”

"Pulled up in a van. They both knew me. I offered them a ride, told them that Neil needed something. They got in willingly."

"And what about their clothes?" I ask.

"Well, I wasn't sure where we would go or what we would do. I knew that their missing posters would be all over the place. It would be a big case in the community, so I wanted them to change. I even colored Violet’s hair. What do you think? Pretty good for an at-home job."

I look at my sister's stringy hair. It's definitely been dyed, but it looks more like something else has happened all together after weeks of not being washed.

I open my mouth to say something else, but he shuts me down.

"Okay. Enough with the questions. I think I've made myself clear. I said way more than I probably should have, but that's because I'm a nice guy and I think that you deserve some answers. Now, it's time to go."

"Go where?"

He takes a step closer and pushes me tighter against the boulder. Violet just cowers slightly in the corner but doesn't really respond.

"We're going on a little trip," he says, and I think I see a twinkle in his eye.

"Where?"

"Well, I know you're not going to want to go back home with me and hang out, and I'm going to have to watch you way too carefully. Why don't we go on a little trip into the desert?"

I plant my feet and don't move.

"Start walking or I'm going to kill her right now."

My heart jumps into my throat and I reach for Violet.

35

I shuffle my feet, trying to slow the process down and come up with a plan. I notice that my feet leave a little trail from the boulder all the way to where we're headed.

But a trail for others to investigate isn't enough right now. I need to figure out a way to stop this. Goss walks with his rifle pointed at Violet, who is still in a somewhat catatonic state. I hold her up, she moves barely, somewhat responding, but not really.

It's like she's in shock.

We are headed to the other side of the fence, closer to the mountain, about half an acre away. We pass a couple of Joshua trees and creosote bushes out to the side.

The thing about the creosote is that even though they're beautiful, they're deadly. Wherever they grow, they suck up all of the energy and water and nutrients from the soil, making it impossible for other plants around them to survive. The bush is tall, magnificent. And if you were to stand behind it, you would hardly be seen.

"Keep going," Goss instructs. And I do as he says, trying to figure out the best way to attack, to turn this around on him.

"Dad, stop!"

Something ricochets above my head.

"Stop! What are you doing?"

I hear the heavy footsteps running up to me, the shuffling of feet against the desert floor.

When I squint into the light, I recognize *him*. It's Neil.

Goss's face turns as white as a sheet. I don't waste a second, launching myself onto him. Jumping onto his back, I push him onto the ground.

The rifle falls somewhere away from us.

I have the upper hand, but I don't stop there. I grab a rock I had spotted right before I heard Neil, one that I debated as to how to pick up without Goss noticing.

I slam it into the back of his head.

Stunned, he starts to reach for the rifle, but I hit him again and then grab his arm, twisting it behind his back. As we tussle, I realize just how strong he is, but he's bleeding from his head.

I hadn't hit him exactly right, causing just a cut instead of a complete disarmament. As he grabs onto me I reach for the rifle. This time I grab it, but I don't have enough space to point it at him.

I hit him with it like it's a baseball bat and he falls flat on the ground. When I take a few steps closer and he reaches for me, I use the butt of the rifle to smash his head in until Neil pulls me away.

Bloodlust is spilling out of me and somewhere in the distance, I hear the cries, "stop it, stop it, stop it."

They belong to Neil. I let him pull me away from his father but keep the rifle pointed at Goss, who lies bloodied on the pale yellow desert rocks.

His face is mashed in. His nose is unrecognizable. Darkness pools around his eyes just below and all around. Still, I keep the rifle fixed on him. Briefly, I turn my hips to look at Neil thinking that he may be the second to attack, but instead I find him cradling Violet, holding her gently in his arms, tears running down his cheeks.

He looks like the child that he is, no older than fourteen.

"What are you doing here?" I ask.

"It was him all along," Neil whispers and starts gasping for breath. "I just... How did I *not* know?"

He rubs his hand softly against Violet's arm, holding her tightly. His jeans are covered in dust, so is his hair and a bit of his face. The nearby creosote bush is splashed with blood.

"What are you doing here, Neil?" I ask, still holding a strong grip on the rifle in case either of them make a move.

"I forgot my backpack in his car and I found a receipt from TJ Maxx for a bunch of women's clothing, junior size. He had had affairs before and I was pissed as hell. I was going to confront him about it and tell him to stop messing around on Mom, but he wasn't home."

"How did *you* get here?" I ask. "You can't drive."

"Took my scooter to the gas station, the last one before Highway 18. Waited around for a bit. Some trucker came along, said he was heading into Yucca Valley and he'd give me a ride."

"That's not safe," I say before he finishes talking and he smirks at me with disdain. "Nevermind. Keep going. So you just decided to come here because of the clothes?"

"I saw them last night and in the middle of the night I walked past their room, Mom and Dad's, and he wasn't there. I knew Mom would just lose it when she woke up. That he'd just have some excuse about where he'd gone. And so I checked the Nest camera and I saw him at the cabin."

"There's a Nest camera pointed at this cabin? To this place?"

"Yeah."

He nods.

"I helped him set it up not too long ago. Actually right around Violet's disappearance. But unlike the one on our house, it just went to his laptop and he said that he didn't need to worry Mom about it."

I'm not sure what Neil knows, but according to Goss, his wife is clueless about this place still being in the family.

“So, what did the Nest camera connect to?" I ask.

"His laptop and his phone. He'd told me the password to his laptop and he forgot about it, I guess, back at the house because I logged in, saw him entering last night. I knew he was here and I was going to catch him having an affair.

"I'm so sorry, Violet. I'm so sorry I didn't come here sooner," Neil says, beginning to cry.

He holds her tightly in his arms and she responds just a little bit, acknowledging his presence.

Goss starts to lift up his head just a little bit and for a moment I consider whether I should pull the trigger.

What if I do? What if I say it slipped? No one would blame me, probably not even Neil himself.

But then I look at Violet and decide *not* to. This man is going to be put on trial.

Natalie's family is going to get justice for what he did. There are still so many unanswered questions and we all deserve to know more.

Somewhere in the distance, I hear the police sirens. The cavalry is coming.

36

Back in LA prior to my trip to Big Bear, I find Amelia in her hotel room completely distraught over Christian's death. I manage to calm her down and get her to take deep breaths and stop hyperventilating. I hold her while she cries and tells me how much she loved him. I am there when she pounds the bed and yells about how much she hated him. I stay with her for hours and make arrangements for the next hotel.

After Christian's suicide, Leonard, Sonny, and his mother, Dolores, are brought in and questioned. Leonard is arrested. During his interrogation, Sonny looks completely baffled and shocked by what happened.

He doesn't want to believe me.

But when I play him clips from our recording, he opens his mouth and starts to talk. He didn't know anything about his father planning Kelly's death but confirms that Leonard did indeed meet with Christian on that day. Sonny remembers how surprised he was since they'd never been in contact much before.

I've had my doubts about Sonny's mother for a long time. Was she a part of it? Was she not? But despite how much I suspected Dolores, we did not have enough evidence to bring a case against her. Unless, of course, Sonny had something to offer, which he did not.

Judging from Sonny's reaction, he thought that Leonard was working on his own. But then again, he'd never suspected his father of being involved with this in the first place. There are certain things that you just don't know the answers to, perhaps you never will, and you just have to be okay with it.

Amelia continues to stay in hiding. The witness protection program gets her approved and ready for a new identity after the trial. Leonard refuses to take any sort of plea deal. All offers required at least twenty years in prison so the case proceeds to jury selection.

Then one random Tuesday, Leonard is found dead in his cell, killed by his cellmate. The rumor is that Sonny ordered the hit, but there's no evidence and no one comes forward. His cellmate is charged and arrested and a trial is set, and he insists that he did it because they had been arguing that day.

I have my suspicions, but no proof.

Sonny ascends to the role of top dog at the motorcycle club and his father gets what was coming to him for killing his wife. I guess that's as much justice as Kelly will get.

Violet is starting to become her old self again. She has had weeks of intensive therapy but she's talking about it a little bit. I stay with her in Mom's house and take a leave of absence to help her adjust a bit. We have fun. We laugh and we never talk about the case.

She doesn't want to. She does enough of that with the therapist and with the prosecutor and everyone else. When I found her at that cabin she was drugged with a high dose of heroin and morphine. She's lucky to be alive.

In addition to all the trauma that she'd experienced, including rape, she now also has a severe drug addiction. As evidence started to be pieced together, we found out that Goss took her and kept her drugged in his cabin all of this time, ever since the first day that she disappeared.

A little bit later, he decided to take Natalie as well. They were both sexually assaulted and then given high doses of heroin to keep them sleeping and calm and not alert while he was gone.

But then something happened. Goss came back one day and Natalie was dead. The autopsy results finally came in. We had suspected a poisoning but it was simpler than that: a fentanyl overdose. It's a powerful synthetic opioid that is thirty to forty times more potent than heroin. It is short acting and cannot be seen, tasted or smelled when mixed into other drugs.

Not wanting to lead prosecutors to this area and to expand the search, Goss decided to dump her body back in Big Bear, hoping that the investigators would think that some local person or a drifter passing through had committed this terrible crime.

He wanted the two cases to be separate and he wanted to keep Violet in that state in his cabin for the foreseeable future. When we investigated more, we found that there was a trap door and a whole secret room underneath the house that was built prior to Violet's kidnapping.

Goss had been planning this. Though he decided to take someone that his family was connected to, everything else was executed quite expertly and kept us searching for clues.

If it weren't for the mistake that he'd made by asking Neil to set up the Nest camera and then having a history of infidelity, we would not be here. If Neil had not decided to hitchhike here, I doubt that anyone would've found my body and Violet would still be living in hell.

She was initially kept in the secret room underneath the house. But when she became more cooperative and he started to trust her more, Goss let her up into the house, which is where I found her, but still tied up and handcuffed. The physical restraints in addition to the drugs made it practically impossible for her to escape.

Later on, I also found out that the place where he was leading us, or perhaps me in particular, was a mine shaft that was located on his property out near the hills. It was a closed mine, one of the ones that someone had set up in the 50s that was no longer operational.

If he had dumped my body there and then pushed it underneath, away from visible sight, even any curious onlookers who would look down into it would not have spotted me and I would never be found.

There are thousands of people who have met this death in the great American West. I would've been one of them.

Luke comes in as Violet and I are curled up on the couch, watching television. Mom is grocery shopping for dinner. Luke is staying here for a few days for a visit. He is caring and delicate with Violet and he's still handling me with kid gloves.

I look over and give him a big smile.

"How are you?" he whispers, trying not to wake up Violet who's curled up on the couch next to me, fast asleep.

"Good," I say, nodding in her direction.

"How's she?" he whispers.

"Better, a lot better. We laughed so hard today. And that is the first time in, well, ages."

"Glad to hear it."

He leans over and gives me a peck on the head.

"I wanted to tell you that I've decided to give a statement to Internal Affairs about Thomas," I say when I sneak out from underneath the blanket and head to the kitchen to put on the kettle for some hot tea.

"Really?"

"Yeah. Catherine did. I know she said it was up to me, and it is, but it's the right thing to do. He shouldn't be on the force any more. They have to know everything that he's capable of because someone's going to get killed if I don't do this."

"I'm proud of you," Luke says, giving me a tight squeeze.

"I don't know why it took me so long to reach this decision and I don't know what's going to happen. People aren't going to like it. It's going to be a 'he said, she said' situation and my colleagues are going to question my motives."

"But it's going to be fine," Luke says. "Besides, you can always come join the FBI. There's going to be an opening."

I chuckle.

"You're really leaving?"

He nods.

"Yeah. It's not for me. I have to figure out something else to do. It's just too much darkness and sadness."

"What about Violet's case?"

"It's a miracle that she was found. But a lot of cases don't up end up like that, as you well know."

I nod.

"Anyway, I think you're doing the right thing, about Thomas."

The tea kettle starts to boil and I pop two green tea bags into our mugs and fill them up to the rim.

"Something else I wanted to ask you," I say.

"Okay." He brings the cup to his lips and gives me that familiar, warm smile.

"Do you prefer May or June?"

"For what?" he asks.

"For our wedding."

"You're really set on that? Are you sure?" he asks. "I'm not trying to pressure you."

"I know. I just think it's time that I move on with my life and do things that make me happy. Marrying you is going to make me incredibly happy."

"Okay. In that case, May," he says.

I smile and shake my head a little bit from side to side.

"What? What's wrong with May?" He acts offended.

"Well, I've always wanted to be a June bride."

"Hey, you asked me. I'm telling you it's going to be May." Luke points a finger in my face.

I grab onto him and pull him close, kissing him hard.

"We're going to be okay, right?" I ask, looking up at him, deep into his eyes.

"Everything's going to be great from now on."

THANK YOU FOR READING! Can't wait to find out what happens next?

1-click Gone too Son (A Detective Kaitlyn Carr Mystery) now!

A letter throws Detective Kaitlyn Carr's life into turmoil...

Settling into a new routine, Kaitlyn believes that her troubles are behind her. But then she receives a letter from a retired FBI agent, which states that everything she knows about her father's death is a lie.

The FBI agent says that her father was murdered and promises to tell her what really happened, but only if she helps him first.

To find out the truth, Kaitlyn must travel to a place with a near-constant cover of clouds and rain and investigate a series of cold cases that the FBI agent believes are connected to the same illusive serial killer.

Here, the foliage is thick. The rains wash away evidence. It's the perfect place to bury bodies, or to leave them somewhere no one will find them.

The FBI agent might be a conspiracy theorist and Kaitlyn isn't sure if she believes any of it until she finds a young woman's bodyand wonders if her murder is also linked to the serial killer.

Deep in the pines and gloom of the Pacific Northwest, Kaitlyn hunts the serial killer, but what she does not yet know is that she might be the one who is being hunted....

1-click Gone too Son (A Detective Kaitlyn Carr Mystery) now!

If you enjoyed this book, please take a moment to write a short review on your favorite book site and maybe recommend it to a friend or two.

Can't wait to read another provocative and suspenseful series?

1-click LAST BREATH now!

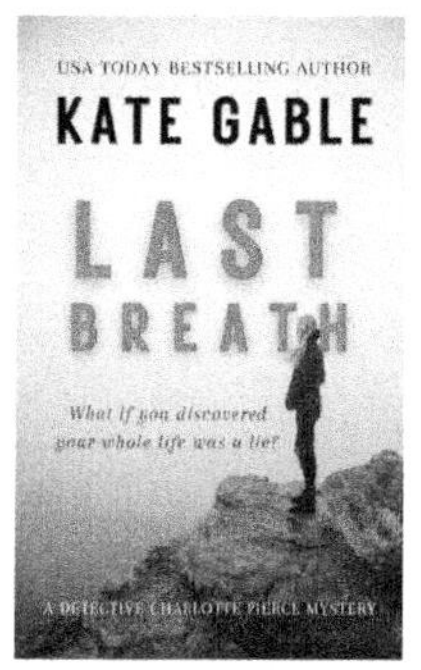

☆☆☆☆☆ *"Gripping! Fascinating mystery thriller filled with intriguing characters and lots of twists and turns!" (Goodreads review for Girl Missing)*

A couple expecting their first child is brutally murdered in their home. The prime suspect is the scorned ex-wife

who supposedly has no knowledge of why she's there or what happened.

When Detective Charlotte Pierce arrives at the scene, it's up to her to unravel the mystery of newlyweds' murder. It looks like an open and shut case, but certain things are not adding up.

Despite pressures from her FBI director father, Charlotte came to Mesquite County to escape the burdens of a big city police department. She has been through a lot and a quiet suburban community where nothing really happens is exactly what she is looking for.

Little does she know that this quiet community is filled with secrets of its own, including those within the police department. She could easily go with the flow, but she refuses to ignore even the smallest inconsistencies.

Was it the ex-wife or is the murderer still out there?

Can Charlotte get to the truth before he kills again?

1-click LAST BREATH now!

CAN'T GET ENOUGH of Kaitlyn Carr? Make sure to grab **GIRL HIDDEN (a novella) for FREE!**

A family is found dead in their home. The only survivor is the teenage daughter who managed to escape the burning house.

Who killed them? And why? **Detective Kaitlyn Carr has to bring their killer to justice.**

A year before her disappearance, Violet, Kaitlyn's sister, comes to stay with her after a bad fight with their mom. She can't stand living at home as much as Kaitlyn once did and wants to move in with her.

What happens when the dysfunction of her own family threatens to blow up her face and let the killer off for good?

GRAB GIRL HIDDEN for FREE now!

If you enjoyed this book, please take a moment to write a short review on your favorite book site and maybe recommend it to a friend or two.

You can also join my Facebook group, Kate Gable's Reader Club, for exclusive giveaways and sneak peeks of future books.

BE THE FIRST TO KNOW ABOUT MY UPCOMING SALES, NEW RELEASES AND EXCLUSIVE GIVEAWAYS!

Want a Free book? Sign up for my Newsletter!

Sign up for my newsletter:

https://www.subscribepage.com/kategableviplist

Join my Facebook Group:
https://www.facebook.com/groups/
833851020557518

Bonus Points: Follow me on BookBub and Goodreads!

https://www.goodreads.com/author/show/
21534224.Kate_Gable

ABOUT KATE GABLE

Kate Gable loves a good mystery that is full of suspense. She grew up devouring psychological thrillers and crime novels as well as movies, tv shows and true crime.

Her favorite stories are the ones that are centered on families with lots of secrets and lies as well as many twists and turns. Her novels have elements of psychological suspense, thriller, mystery and romance.

Kate Gable lives near Palm Springs, CA with her husband, son, a dog and a cat. She has spent more than twenty years in Southern California and finds inspiration from its cities, canyons, deserts, and small mountain towns.

She graduated from University of Southern California with a Bachelor's degree in Mathematics. After pursuing graduate studies in mathematics, she switched gears and got her MA in Creative Writing and English from Western New Mexico University and her PhD in Education from Old Dominion University.

Writing has always been her passion and obsession. Kate is also a USA Today Bestselling author of romantic suspense under another pen name.

Write her here:

Kate@kategable.com

Check out her books here:

www.kategable.com

Sign up for my newsletter:
https://www.subscribepage.com/kategableviplist

Join my Facebook Group:
https://www.facebook.com/groups/833851020557518

Bonus Points: Follow me on BookBub and Goodreads!

https://www.bookbub.com/authors/kate-gable

https://www.goodreads.com/author/show/21534224.Kate_Gable

amazon.com/Kate-Gable/e/B095XFCLL7
facebook.com/kategablebooks
bookbub.com/authors/kate-gable
instagram.com/kategablebooks

ALSO BY KATE GABLE

Detective Kaitlyn Carr Psychological Mystery series

Girl Missing (Book 1)
Girl Lost (Book 2)
Girl Found (Book 3)
Girl Taken (Book 4)
Girl Forgotten (Book 5)
Gone Too Soon (Book 6)
Gone Forever (Book 7)
Whispers in the Sand (Book 8)

Girl Hidden (FREE Novella)

Detective Charlotte Pierce Psychological Mystery series

Last Breath

Nameless Girl
Missing Lives
Girl in the Lake

Printed in Great Britain
by Amazon